A legend begins

Maybe it was just a combination of the odd lighting and the smoky air, but Luke seemed to have a glow around him, an almost surreal bluish haze. He clutched the microphone and began to sing.

When it was over, Juliet saw with alarm that Dani's face was drained of color.

"I know him," she whispered.

Juliet gaped. "You mean you know who he is? You've seen him before?"

"It's Luke," Dani said.

"He's *like* Luke," Juliet began carefully, but at that moment waves of applause drowned her out. This usually blasé audience was going berserk, not just with clapping but with hoots, whistles, and even screams.

Loud as it was, though, Juliet heard Dani's next words with frightening clarity.

"I always knew he wasn't dead. He *couldn't* be."

D1251564

DREAM LOVER

DREAM LOVER

by
Marilyn
Kaye

WESTWIND
Troll Associates

For Christophe Fontaine
(enfin, ton livre)

Text copyright © 1995 by Marilyn Kaye.
Cover illustration copyright © 1995 by Joanie Schwarz.

Published by Troll Associates, Inc. WestWind is a trademark of Troll Associates.

Printed in the United States of America.

10 9 8 7 6 5 4 3 2 1

CHAPTER · 1

At precisely 8:00 P.M., Juliet Turner pulled back her bedroom curtain and peered out. The dim street light didn't offer much illumination, but she could still appreciate the cold, still beauty of the winter night. She never tired of the sight, despite the fact that in Chicago, the first snow always seemed to fall over the Thanksgiving weekend. It was now February, and eighteen years of experience assured her she could probably count on this sight until Easter.

A moment later, a familiar car came up the street, slowing as it reached her house. The headlights hit the snow, exposing the blue white sheen. Then the car pulled into the driveway, and the driver looked up toward the second-floor window. Juliet waved, the boy behind the wheel saluted, and she let the curtain drop.

She went to the mirror and rubbed a spot under her eye where her mascara had smeared. She checked the contents of her purse, noting the wallet, keys, and lipstick. Then she hurried out and ran down the stairs.

At the bottom, she paused and rapped lightly on the door off the alcove. Without waiting for an acknowledgment of her knock, she pushed the door open.

"Dad? Keith's here. I'm leaving."

The man sitting at the antique wooden desk raised his head. His vague, gentle eyes focused on her briefly. "Have a nice time."

"Now, don't forget, you're expected at the Cranstons' tonight. Mr. Cranston's retirement party. I'm leaving the car for you. Dad!"

She waited for the light of comprehension to come into his eyes. "Yes, Juliet, I'll remember. And thank you for reminding me."

"I won't be late," she assured him, even though he hadn't indicated any anxiety. She always said that anyway.

She closed the door, and smiled. Just the day before, she'd been at her friend Dani's house. They were heading out for a movie, but before they could leave, Dani was subjected to an interrogation by her parents: where are you going, how are you getting there, what time will you be home.

"You're so lucky," Dani told her later, knowing that Juliet never had to endure that sort of grilling. And Juliet had to agree. Of course, her father knew she would take care of herself. Unlike Dani's parents, who were entitled to express a certain amount of concern.

She pulled her coat and scarf out of the hall closet, put them on, and left. As she slipped into

8

the car, Keith inclined his face toward her. She leaned over, kissed him briefly, and then settled back, adjusting her seat belt.

Keith pulled out of the driveway. They moved along the street lined with bare trees and old houses, and then past the Gothic-style buildings of the University of Chicago.

"How was your day?" he asked.

"Fine," she replied. "The usual. It's funny, though, I can't remember one word that was said in any of my classes. It seems like that's the way it is everyday lately."

"You're treading water," Keith said. "It was the same for me, the last semester of my senior year. That's the way it is for everyone, I think. You put your brain on automatic pilot and you cruise."

"Exactly," Juliet agreed. "I feel like I'm just going through the motions. Last spring was different. Studying for the S.A.T.s, filling out those college applications . . . I was so tense all the time."

"I remember," Keith said dryly. "Very well."

"You couldn't blame me for feeling like that. My whole life was at stake!" She grinned. "I must have been a real pain to be around."

"That's putting it mildly."

She glanced at him curiously. "Why did you put up with all that?"

"Because I knew you'd breeze through the S.A.T.s, you'd get into the school of your choice, and then you'd be your old self again."

He knew her so well. "Yeah. It's good having everything settled, and knowing exactly what the next few years are going to be like."

"Do you ever wish you were going away to school, leaving Chicago?" he asked her.

"Not really. I guess it would be interesting to go someplace different, but it wouldn't make sense for me." She ticked off the reasons on her fingers. "If I want to go into anthropology, the University of Chicago is the place to be. And with my father on the faculty, I get free tuition. I can live at home, and I can keep my part-time job at the bookstore and save money so that maybe I can spend my junior year studying abroad."

Keith nodded in approval. "Sounds like you've got it all figured out. But can I assume those aren't the only reasons you're staying in town?"

"Oh, I suppose there are other benefits," she teased. "Like not having to scrounge around for someone new to go out with." Keith was maneuvering around a pothole, so he didn't look at her, but his broad smile was reassuring. After almost a year together, Keith was another part of the future she could count on.

"How was *your* day?" she asked. "Did you meet with Professor what's-his-name, the famous one?"

"Robbins, yeah. He says my proposal's exciting, and he thinks I can get funding for the research from his grant."

"That's great." She didn't ask for any more details, and Keith didn't offer them. Early on in their relationship, she'd asked him about his work and he'd tried to explain, but she found chemical engineering impossible to comprehend. All she knew was that the engineering school at North-western was considered to be one of the best and one of the toughest in the country. She respected Keith's work, but she was grateful that he didn't expect her to understand it.

"So I spent all afternoon in the library, going through journals," Keith continued.

"And I'll bet you haven't eaten all day," Juliet scolded.

"Not since lunch," Keith admitted. "I missed dinner at the frat house."

"You should have come eaten with us. It was the housekeeper's day off, so I fixed dinner. Linguini with goat cheese and sun-dried tomatoes."

"Sounds super. Did your father appreciate it?"

"Are you kidding? He never knows what he's eating. When he remembers to eat, that is. Sometimes I think he'd starve to death if someone didn't put food in front of him."

"Is he still working on that revision of his literature anthology?"

"Yes." Juliet shook her head ruefully. "Honestly, the house could burn down around him and they'd find him still sitting at his desk, trying to choose between two poems."

"Was he like this when your mother was alive?" Keith asked.

"Probably." Juliet thought for a moment. She had been only five when her mother died. Juliet had only dim flashes of memory from that time, but yes, even then, her father hadn't been much more than a pleasant, nondemanding presence,

11

occasionally reading aloud to her poems she couldn't possibly have understood.

"He's not that unusual, for an academic type," she added. "I've known professors like that all my life. A lot of them are out of touch with the real world. But they're happy, and they don't do any harm . . ."

"You don't have to defend him," Keith said. "I guess engineering professors are more down-to-earth. Maybe that's why I fit in so well."

Juliet gazed at him appreciatively. Yes, Keith definitely was in touch with the real world. Maybe that was one of the reasons she found him so appealing. She felt like she was on solid ground with Keith.

Keith had turned onto Lake Shore Drive, the stretch of road that went along the side of the city. The road could be tricky in winter, and he had to concentrate. Juliet settled back in her seat. She liked watching Keith drive. His expression was serious, determined.

Normally, Juliet was only at ease in a car when she herself was driving. She liked being in control. Whenever she and Dani went anywhere, Juliet insisted on driving.

But with Keith, she could relax. In fact, if she had to come up with one word to describe their year together, *relaxing* would be the word she'd choose. Other words popped into her head. *Comfortable. Warm. Secure.* There had been guys in her life before Keith, but never one who could make her feel so calm. Like being wrapped in a cozy quilt on a cold night.

The image made her feel sleepy, and she half-closed her eyes. Maybe that was why Keith saw the figure first. They were moving along slowly, avoiding icy patches, when he said, "Juliet, look. Up ahead, to the right."

She opened her eyes. Someone was walking along the side of the highway. Actually, *walking* wasn't the right word. He was staggering, dangerously close to the road.

"Drunk?" Juliet suggested.

"On Lake Shore Drive? How did he get across it?"

Keith had a point. To the left of them lay the near north side of Chicago, with its restaurants and nightlife. But on the right, beyond the highway, there was only Lake Michigan.

Keith carefully steered the car onto the rim of the highway and came to a halt. The person was just a few yards in front of them, caught in the beam of their headlights. They were close enough now to get a good look at him.

He was young, probably no older than Keith. Dark, tangled hair stopped just short of his shoulders. He was slender, dressed in jeans, tight ones, and a shirt. He stopped walking, but his body listed slightly to one side.

"He must be freezing," Juliet murmured.

"Maybe he's been in an accident," Keith said. "You'd better stay here." He got out of the car. Juliet rolled down a window to listen.

"Do you need some help?" Keith called out as he

13

made his way toward him.

The boy mumbled something that was inaudible to Juliet. He moved to get past Keith, but he stumbled, and Keith grabbed his arm. "Are you okay? Where's your car?"

His head jerked up and he looked around wildly. Then his shoulders slumped. He put a hand to his head.

Despite Keith's warning, Juliet got out of the car. "What's the problem?"

"I think he's been hurt," Keith replied.

As she drew closer, Juliet sniffed, but she couldn't detect the scent of liquor on him. "Are you high on something?" she asked bluntly.

He raised his head. There was definitely something wrong with him, but his eyes weren't glazed over. To Juliet's mind, he didn't seem stoned. More like—lost. Again he touched the side of his head.

"I think he's got a concussion or something," Keith said. "Come on, fellow, we'll take you to a hospital."

The boy offered no resistance as Keith took one arm, Juliet took the other, and they led him to the car. They eased him into the backseat.

Keith started the car up again. "Where's the closest emergency room?" he wondered out loud.

"No!"

It was the first recognizable word the boy had uttered. Juliet and Keith turned around to face him.

"Please . . . I don't want to go to the hospital."

"But you're hurt," Keith said. "You need help."

14

He gave his head a nearly imperceptible shake and then winced from the effort. "No . . . I'll be okay. Really. I . . . I just want to go home. Will you drive me home?"

Juliet and Keith looked at each other. "We can't force him to go to a hospital," Juliet said in a low voice. "Maybe there's someone at his home who can take care of him."

Keith shrugged. He turned back to face him. "Okay, we'll take you home. Where do you live?"

There was a silence from the back seat. Juliet turned. The boy's mouth was slightly open, and he seemed to be struggling for words.

And when he finally spoke, his voice was as small as a child's.

"I don't know."

CHAPTER · 2

There was a moment of silence. Then Keith said, "What's your name?"

The boy repeated, "I don't know."

"Look in your pockets," Juliet instructed. "You must have a wallet or something."

The boy reached into both pockets and pulled them inside out. There was nothing there, not even loose change.

A truck passed, narrowly missing sideswiping Keith's car. Keith drove back onto the highway, and they continued to head north. Juliet loosened her seat belt so she could get a better view of their passenger in the backseat. "You really should see a doctor," she said.

"I feel all right."

"But you don't even know your name! There's something wrong with you."

"What's the last thing you remember?" Keith asked.

"Just being there. On that road."

Juliet studied him. The panic seemed to be gone

16

from his face, but there wasn't enough light in the car for her to get a clear sense of his feelings. "You don't remember how you got there?"

"No."

"Do you know where you are now?"

He shook his head.

"Chicago." She pronounced the word slowly, enunciating every syllable. "Does that mean anything to you? Do you live here?"

He shrugged.

Keith broke in. "Juliet, don't put the poor guy through the Inquisition!"

Juliet persisted. "Do you know anything at all about Chicago?"

She could have sworn a faint smile creased his face for a moment. "It's in Illinois."

"There!" she declared triumphantly. "You *do* know some things."

"I know lots of things," he said. His voice was soft and even. "States and capitals, rivers and mountains . . . but unfortunately, I don't know anything about myself."

"Selective amnesia," Keith stated. "I've read about that. It's not uncommon after a blow to the head. I think it's supposed to wear off."

Still staring, Juliet spoke to Keith. "What are we going to do with him?"

Again she saw that hint of a smile, and she flushed. She was talking about him as if he couldn't understand what she was saying.

Keith had better manners. "We'll take you to my fraternity house. With luck, your memory will come

17

back in the next few hours, and then we can take you home."

The boy made no objection, and the rest of the ride to Northwestern was quiet.

Gamma house was lit up, and as they all got out of the car, they could hear the music coming from the basement. Inside, the floor of the living room vibrated from the noise downstairs. The boy was walking fine on his own now, and he followed them upstairs to Keith's room.

"Why don't you lie down on my bed?" Keith suggested. The boy complied. Now that Juliet had the opportunity to get a good look at him, she couldn't bring herself to do it. Every time she glanced at him, his eyes met hers directly, and she found herself looking away.

A couple of Keith's fraternity brothers appeared at the door. "What's up?" one of them asked. "Hi, Juliet."

"Hi, Gary, John."

Keith indicated the prone figure. "We found this guy on the Drive. He hit his head, I think, or someone hit it for him. Anyway, he doesn't know who he is or where he lives. I figured I'd let him lie here for a while and see if his memory comes back. If not . . ."

Gary whistled. "Amnesia, huh? I've never seen that in real life." He gazed at the boy with unconcealed interest.

"He doesn't have a wallet or any ID?" John asked.

Keith shook his head. "Maybe he was robbed."

18

"And the robber hit him on the head," Juliet added.

The boy spoke to Gary, who was still staring at him. "Have you seen me before?"

Gary scratched his head. "I don't think so. But you remind me of someone." His forehead puckered, and then he shrugged. "You guys coming down to the party?"

"Yeah," Keith replied. But he looked at the boy on the bed and hesitated.

The boy drew himself up. "Look, don't worry about me. I'll just lie here for a while, and then I'll take off."

"You should eat something first," Juliet remarked. As she spoke, she looked at him. His blue eyes were so clear, they seemed to be transparent. She looked away.

"That's a good idea," Keith said. "I'll go downstairs and see what I can round up."

"I'll stay here with him," Juliet said. Keith nodded, and left with Gary and John.

The boy spoke. "You don't have to stay here with me."

"It's okay." Juliet began to move around the room. She picked up some books from the floor and stacked them on Keith's desk. She took a shirt off of the back of a chair and hung it up in the closet.

"Your name's Juliet?"

"Yes."

"As in Romeo and?"

"My father's an English professor," she

explained.

"And the guy, Keith . . . he's your boyfriend?"

"Yes."

"Nice guy."

"He is." She found herself wishing for that nice guy to hurry back. Not that she felt she was in any danger. The boy hadn't stirred from his position, the door was open, and people were constantly passing by.

But she sensed his eyes following her around the room. And when she glanced in his direction, her sensation was confirmed.

She turned her back to him and straightened a framed photo on the wall.

"Pretty picture," he said.

"It's a beach, in Mexico. We went there last spring." Then, ever so casually, she asked, "Ever been there?"

"Maybe."

She turned and looked at him sharply.

"Or maybe not. I wouldn't know, would I?"

She stiffened. Was he teasing her? But those eyes, those see-through eyes, were completely innocent.

Keith returned, bearing a tray. "I've got nachos here, and potato chips . . ."

Juliet rolled her eyes. "Nachos and potato chips? Very healthful."

Keith defended the selections. "Hey, it's a party down there. What did you expect, granola and yogurt?" He placed the tray on the bed.

"Looks great to me," the boy said.

"There's an empty room next door," Keith went on. "Why don't you plan on staying the night here?"

"Thanks. Hey, you guys don't have to hang around and baby-sit me. Go join your party."

Keith nodded. "Feel free to watch TV, or whatever. We'll be down in the basement if you need anything." He followed Juliet out the door.

"Are you sure it's okay, leaving him alone in your room?" she asked.

"Why not?"

"We don't know anything about this guy. This amnesia thing could be a ruse. He might be a thief or something."

"You're such a skeptic," Keith remarked. "That's what comes from growing up in the big city." He gazed at her fondly.

"And you're being so naive," she retorted with equal affection.

He grinned. "I was raised on a farm. There was never any reason to distrust the cows. Do you think this guy is up to something suspicious?"

"No, I guess not. Still, there's something about him. When Gary said he looked familiar, I started thinking I'd seen him before, too."

"Where? On a wanted poster in the post office?"

"It's possible." She relented. "Okay, probably not. I never look at those things."

They entered the basement, where the party was in full swing. Keith had to raise his voice to be heard. "If it makes you feel better, I'll check on him later. And I'll tell a couple of the guys to look in, too."

21

Juliet nodded. Then she resolutely pushed the amnesiac from her mind. She danced, she talked, she ate, and, as always, she kept an eye open for available men to fix Dani up with.

Keith was true to his word. He spoke to John and Gary, who both agreed to look in on the boy. When Gary returned from his tour of duty, he joined Juliet and Keith on the sofa.

"That's an interesting guy," he commented.

"Has he remembered anything?" Juliet asked.

"No. He doesn't seem all that worried about it, either."

"He'll probably be fine in the morning," Keith said.

Juliet was curious. "What did you talk about with him?"

Gary reddened. "It was weird. I was just making small talk, but somehow we ended up—*I* ended up telling him about myself. Personal stuff. Don't know why."

"I'll bet he's a good listener," Keith remarked.

"Yeah, how did you know?"

"It's logical. If he has no memory, he can't have much to say about himself, so what can he do besides listen?"

"But he *did* talk," Gary said. "He gave me some good advice, too."

Keith's eyebrows shot up. "You asked a total stranger for advice? Hey, I'm hurt, man!"

Gary laughed. "Sometimes it's easier to talk to strangers than friends." He got up. "I wouldn't mind if this guy stuck around for a while."

"Don't count on it," Keith advised him. "By tomorrow, he'll remember that he's got a life somewhere."

Later, Juliet recalled those words as Keith drove her home. "What if he doesn't?"

"What if who doesn't what?"

"What if that guy doesn't regain his memory tomorrow?"

"We'll worry about it tomorrow," Keith replied easily. "You're coming over, aren't you?"

"Sure. I'm shopping with Dani in the afternoon, but I'll be over by six." She paused. "Imagine, not even knowing your own name. Although I wouldn't mind forgetting mine."

He pulled into her driveway and stopped the car. "What's wrong with 'Juliet'?"

"Everyone automatically thinks 'Romeo and.' It's so, I don't know, romantic."

"There's nothing wrong with that." His voice was husky. Automatically, Juliet undid her seat belt and moved closer. He wrapped his arms around her, she buried herself in his broad chest and snuggled close.

After a few minutes, she whispered, "Do you want to come in? I'm sure Dad's asleep."

"Not tonight," he said with obvious reluctance. "I'm beat."

"Yeah, me too."

He walked her to the door. It was too cold to kiss for very long.

Up in her room, Juliet turned on the bedside lamp. She'd lied to Keith. She wasn't tired, not at all. If anything, the odd events of the evening had left her feeling almost hyper. As she undressed, she thought about her shopping jaunt tomorrow. She'd been thinking about redecorating this room, making it more collegiate, less high-school. Maybe getting some new posters.

It was then that it hit her. She turned to look at the picture that she had tacked to her wall four years ago.

It wasn't an uncommon poster. The image would be instantly recognizable to anyone with the most remote familiarity with rock music of the 1960s.

She moved closer. Dani had the same poster in her room. They'd bought them together. Today, they prided themselves on the fact that they'd been turned on to Luke Dennison long before the current revival of interest in his music.

She examined the angular face with its pouting mouth and clear blue eyes, framed by shoulder-length, tangled brown curls. Yes, this was who the stranger reminded her of—Luke Dennison. There was a definite resemblance.

Amazing, she thought. She couldn't wait to tell Dani. They used to fantasize about meeting Luke Dennison, being swept away by the tempestuous rock star into his private wild and reckless world. And they'd sighed over the futility of their fantasies—impossible dreams, not simply because he was a rock star, but because he was dead. Long dead, before either of them were even born. What would Dani say when she heard that a real live guy existed who actually looked like Luke Dennison? It would be all Juliet could do to restrain her from tearing off for the Gamma house at Northwestern.

At age fourteen, their passion for Luke Dennison had been remarkable. They'd argued over who was better suited to him.

"I'm more his type," Dani had insisted. "We're both rebels. *You*—you'd be nagging him to brush his teeth." She was probably right. Still, Juliet had read everything she could get her hands on about him. She'd pored through old magazines in secondhand bookstores, searching for articles, and she'd reveled in reports of his manic, frenzied life. When Dani went to Rome on a holiday with her parents, Juliet had begged her to photograph Luke's grave. Dani hadn't wanted to. She claimed she didn't want to see a confirmation of his nonexistence. But she'd obliged, and Juliet still had the photo.

Impulsively, Juliet went through her CDs, and picked out *Luke Dennison's Greatest Hits*. She turned the volume low and slipped into bed. But she didn't turn off the light right away.

It had been a while since she'd listened to these songs. She'd almost forgotten how the melodies pierced her skin and made her shiver, how the lyrics made her want to shriek "Yes! Exactly!"

And she began to have the kind of fantasies she hadn't indulged in for years, the image of herself as some sort of free spirit, dancing madly, running wildly, with all the reckless abandon that had nothing to do with her real self. What was it about him, his music, that had the power to liberate this secret, private fantasy?

She sat up in bed suddenly. What kind of silliness was this? She wasn't fourteen years old anymore. It was one thing to get silly and giddy over a dead rock star when you were just a fuzzy-headed kid. It was ridiculous now. Even though no one would ever know, she felt foolish having indulged in such nonsense.

But her eyes moved to the poster, and the face on the poster returned her gaze. That was something she'd loved about this particular pose— the way Luke Dennison's eyes met hers, no matter where she was in the room.

She must have been more tired than she thought. She rested her head on the pillow, reached out and turned off the light. The room was totally dark now. But she thought about eyes, clear, blue eyes, that followed her all the way to sleep.

CHAPTER · 3

"**A**mnesia?" Dani's spoonful of chili hovered in midair, but her mouth remained open. "You're not serious!"

It was almost three o'clock—late for lunch, but the trendy restaurant was still crowded. The couple at the next table glanced in their direction. Juliet lowered her voice in the hope that Dani would do the same. "That's what Keith calls it. Selective amnesia."

"Never heard of it," Dani pronounced. "I mean, except on soap operas."

Juliet shrugged. "The guy doesn't know who he is or how he ended up on Lake Shore Drive last night. What else are you going to call it?"

"A con game," Dani replied darkly. "A scam." She pointed a stern finger at Juliet. "This so-called amnesiac is halfway cross country right now, in some Gamma brother's car, with a stereo system in the trunk."

Juliet considered this. "That was my first reaction," she admitted. "But Keith thinks he's telling the truth, and he's pretty good at sizing people up."

"What's he like?" Dani asked.

"It's hard to say. Polite. Quiet." She leaned forward. "You're not going to believe who he looks like. Luke Dennison."

Dani almost choked on her chili. "You're kidding," she sputtered.

"No, really, he does. It didn't hit me until I got home and looked at that old poster."

"Luke Dennison," Dani breathed. She began fiddling with a lock of wiry black hair. "I haven't thought about him in ages."

"Don't chew on your hair," Juliet scolded. "And don't tell me you haven't thought about Luke Dennison in ages. I'll bet you still have fantasies about him."

"And you don't?" Dani retorted. She sighed. "No, I guess you don't, now that you've got Keith." Listlessly, she stirred her chili. "Maybe that's why I can't meet a guy I like. I'm waiting for Luke Dennison."

"Who's been dead for twenty years," Juliet interjected.

Dani continued as if she hadn't spoken. "And I can't find anyone who lives up to his standard. Maybe I should meet your amnesiac."

"He's not *my* amnesiac. Besides, like you said, he's probably long gone. And *not* with anyone's car. He's probably recovered his memory by now and gone back to wherever he came from."

"Mmm." Dani was still stirring the chili. "Luke

Dennison. I remember when I went to the cemetery in Rome. It was so weird, all those ancient hippies putting bottles of wine and marijuana joints on his grave."

Juliet shuddered. "Like they were waiting for him to rise from the dead."

"They were paying tribute," Dani said. "Luke Dennison . . . he was magic."

Juliet understood, but, as usual, Dani was getting carried away. "He was also a drunk," she reminded her. "And a junkie. And—"

"A poet," Dani countered. "And a dreamer, and a lover."

Juliet gave up. There was no point getting into an argument over a dead rock star. It was time to change the subject.

"I still have to buy a gift for your sister's baby shower tomorrow. Do you have any idea what she wants or needs?"

Dani grimaced. "Who knows, who cares."

"Dani!"

"I know, it's rotten of me, but I'm so sick of hearing about Mary and Donald and the baby, the new house . . ." She smiled ruefully. "I guess I'm jealous. *She's* got a life." There was a catch in her voice, and Juliet could tell she was dangerously close to tears. She leaned in closer.

"You've got a life, Dani. You just have to decide what you want to do with it."

"That's easy for you to say. You've got Keith. If I had a guy—"

Juliet broke in and spoke briskly. "You can't wait

for a guy to come along and put meaning into your life. You have to do that for yourself."

"Don't give me one of your feminist lectures," Dani snapped. Then she bit her lip. "Sorry. I know, you're right." She drummed her fingers on the table. "I have to get out of Chicago. I want to go somewhere, do something." She fluttered her hands restlessly, as if to illustrate her words.

"You *are* going somewhere," Juliet said. "You're going to the University of Illinois in September, remember?"

"I may not go. I mean, think about it. Downstate Illinois. What can I possibly find there?"

Juliet didn't know what to say. They'd had conversations like this before, discussions that went nowhere. She was torn between pity and frustration. It was worrisome to see her best friend feeling so confused. But it was annoying, too, and Juliet had to take pains to keep that annoyance out of her voice.

"Dani, you've been talking like this for ages, and it's time to start making some decisions."

"I want something to happen to me," Dani mumbled.

"Then *make* it happen!" She stopped when Dani clenched her fists. And she was taken aback when Dani pushed aside her barely touched chili, so violently that the white tablecloth was splattered with red sauce.

"You think I'm pathetic, don't you? You think I can't make decisions? Just watch."

Juliet did, with growing apprehension. She had

no idea what to expect. Dani's scenes were legendary.

Dani rose from her seat, and Juliet steeled herself. A waitress approached. "Can I get you something?"

Dani turned to her with an unreadable expression. "Yes," she hissed. And then, "Can we have the check, please?"

"Sure, right away."

Dani plopped back down in her seat and grinned. "You should see your face. What did you think I was going to do, scream?"

Juliet let out her breath. "Very funny. I thought you were on the verge of a nervous breakdown."

Dani looked around at the now nearly empty restaurant. "Nah, I'd want a bigger audience for that."

"Honestly, Dani, sometimes I could just shake you."

"You're the one who needs some shaking up," Dani retorted.

"What's that supposed to mean?" Juliet demanded.

"Well, look at you. You're so organized, so structured. And you want everyone else to be like that."

Juliet rolled her eyes. "All I did was suggest that you start thinking about what you want to do. If you don't want to go to the U of I, fine, but you'd better come up with an alternative."

"Maybe I don't want to make a plan for the rest of my life, like you." She cocked her head to one side and scrutinized Juliet. "I'll bet you know exactly what you're going to do when we leave this restaurant."

Juliet didn't try to deny it. "I'm going to find a gift for your sister. Then I want to go to that shoe store on Halsted and see if the lined snow boots are still on sale. After that, I'll take the El up to Northwestern and meet Keith. We'll have dinner at the Gamma house, and then we'll probably go to a movie."

As she recited her schedule, Dani shook her head sadly. "Don't you see? You haven't allowed one minute for anything unpredictable to happen."

"I don't *want* anything unpredictable to happen," Juliet replied. "So I'm responsible and organized. Is that a crime? If anything, I deserve credit for it! Do you know what I was doing the other day? Interviewing housekeepers, because my father's too vague and impractical to do it right. How many girls my age can handle that kind of responsibility?"

"Yeah, okay, I give you credit for your maturity. But don't you ever want to let loose, go nuts, do something wild and crazy?"

Juliet was spared having to answer by the arrival of the check. She picked it up. "Do you want to just split this?"

Leaving the restaurant, she avoided looking at Dani. After all these years of friendship, one would think she'd be accustomed to Dani's erratic behavior. Five years of off-and-on therapy hadn't had much impact on her friend. Sometimes Juliet actually enjoyed Dani's edge, the manic side of her up-and-down personality. Back in the days when they'd had their crushes on Luke Dennison, for example, it was Dani who'd invented the outrageous fantasies and fueled Juliet's own enthusiasm. And, she had to admit, she liked the fact that Dani depended on her to keep her from going off the deep end.

But sometimes Dani's mood swings could be unsettling. In five minutes at the restaurant table, she had gone from normal to depressed to angry to silly to argumentative. She couldn't decide whether Dani was becoming even more volatile, or if she herself had become so stable that she couldn't deal with her friend's craziness.

Just thinking about it all was making her uncomfortable. She turned her attention to practical matters. "Now, *what* am I going to get Mary?" They were passing a bookstore, and Juliet paused. "What about a book on baby care?"

"She's probably got them all," Dani mumbled, but they went inside. There was a whole section labeled *Parenting*.

"Have they picked out names?" Juliet asked, studying the shelves.

"I don't know," Dani replied listlessly. "I don't think so."

"How about a baby-name book?" She took one off the shelf and flipped through the pages. "This looks okay. What do you think?"

But Dani had wandered off to the other side of the room. Juliet noticed a slight tear in the book's jacket, so she exchanged it for another copy and took it to the counter.

Dani appeared behind her in line. She, too, was clutching a book. "Look what I found." She held it up so Juliet could see the cover.

"*Out of Control,*" Juliet read aloud. "*A New and Revealing Look into the Life and Death of Luke Dennison.*"

Dani beamed happily. "Hearing you talk about your amnesiac put him back in my head again."

It was on the tip of Juliet's tongue to suggest that they were both well beyond the stage of devouring sensationalism about a rock star. But she didn't want to be responsible for dousing the flicker of joy in Dani's eyes.

"Cool," she said. "But quit calling him *my* amnesiac."

They paid for their books and left. "I'm heading back to Hyde Park," Dani said. "I've got a date tonight."

"I don't believe this," Juliet declared. "We've just spent four hours together, and you're only now getting around to telling me you have a date tonight."

"Blind date. No big deal. Some sophomore from De Paul who's working part-time with my brother-in-law." She made a face. "He's probably a computer nerd, just like Donald."

"Hey, try being optimistic for a change," Juliet urged.

"Have fun at the Gamma house. If the amnesiac's got his memory back, find out if he's got a

34

girlfriend." Dani strode off, but she paused at the corner and turned back. "And find out if he can sing."

Juliet waved. "See you at the shower tomorrow."

She pulled her coat closer and watched as Dani disappeared around the corner. The shoe store was in the opposite direction, but she didn't move. She wasn't really in the mood to try on snow boots.

She looked at her watch. Keith would be at the library for at least another hour. But the guys at Gamma house wouldn't mind if she hung around there. And, she had to admit, she was curious to find out what had become of the amnesiac.

She trudged through the slush to the elevated train platform. Once aboard the train, she realized with some dismay that she'd neglected to put anything to read in her purse. The book she'd bought for Dani's sister wasn't much help. She didn't want to spend thirty minutes studying the meaning and origin of names.

So there was nothing to do but daydream—a pastime she'd never been very good at. She decided to entertain herself by guessing at the amnesiac's identity. When she got to the frat house, she could find out how close she'd come.

But it was too easy. Given his appearance and age, he was most likely a student. Taking into consideration the location where they'd found him, he was probably a student at De Paul. So much for that. Just as Dani had often told her, she didn't have much imagination.

She stirred in her seat and gazed out at the

passing rooftops. Dani . . . *was* she getting worse? Every time Juliet was with her, she felt like she was being taken for a ride on an emotional roller coaster. It wasn't a sensation she appreciated. She didn't even like thinking about it. Luckily, the person sitting next to her got off at the next stop and left his newspaper behind.

The sun was going down by the time she reached Gamma house. Nearing the walkway, she hesitated. Only once before had she walked through the front door alone, and it made her feel uncomfortable, as though she were an intruder. But as she approached the door it opened, as if in anticipation of her arrival.

"Hi, Juliet."

"Hi, John. Is Keith here? He's expecting me," she added quickly.

"I haven't seen him, but he might be in the TV room." With a wave, he moved on past her.

"John!"

He turned.

"That guy we brought here last night . . . did he get his memory back?"

"I don't think so. He's still around."

She went into the house. The formal living room was deserted, but she could hear a low murmur of conversation coming from the TV room beyond. She slipped off her coat, unwound her scarf, and put them in the closet. Then she made her way in the direction of the voices.

There were only two people in the room. The TV was on, but neither Gary nor the amnesiac were watching it. Their backs were to Juliet, and she stood there uncertainly, not wanting to interrupt what seemed to be a serious conversation.

"We've got this band," Gary was saying. "I'm lead guitar. We play local gigs, bars, and high schools, that sort of thing. And when I'm playing, I get this feeling that this is what I want to do always, what I'm supposed to be doing. Not go to law school, not spend my life pushing papers in my father's firm . . ."

"Then don't go to law school. Trust your instincts. Commit yourself to the band."

Juliet coughed softly. The boys turned.

"Sorry. I was looking for Keith . . ." she began.

"He's still in the library," Gary said. "Come on in."

"I don't want to interrupt."

"No, it's okay." Gary nodded toward his companion. "Our friend here thinks I should forget about law school and devote myself to the band. What do you think?"

"Can't you do both?" Juliet asked. "Go to law school and play with the band in your spare time?"

Gary looked at the stranger. For the first time since her arrival, so did Juliet.

He certainly didn't look like he was suffering any ill consequences from whatever he'd endured the night before. His eyes were clear and sharp, almost piercing.

"A hobby," he said. "A pleasant little weekend amusement. Is that what your music means to you?"

"No," Gary said.

"But you have to be practical," Juliet declared. "How are you going to make a living playing in a local band?"

"It doesn't have to stay local," Gary began.

"But how many bands make it big?" Juliet persisted. "I've heard your band, Gary, and I think you're terrific, but there are zillions of bands like that, aren't there? I mean, what are your chances, really?"

Gary nodded. "Yeah, you're probably right."

"So you admit defeat even before you go into battle."

"What's that supposed to mean?" Juliet asked. "All I'm saying is that most bands don't end up becoming the Rolling Stones. There isn't that much room at the top."

"So we impose our own limitations on ourselves. The world doesn't fail us. We fail ourselves." The stranger's voice was soft, gentle, but Gary seemed stung by his words.

Juliet spoke up sharply. "It's not very logical to go into a battle that you can't win."

The boy's eyes bore into her own, though his words were directed at Gary. "Anyone with half a brain can be a lawyer. The world will be no better, no worse, with one less or one more. But music . . . music makes connections, it reaches the soul. Music can make a difference."

What nonsense, Juliet thought. Like one rock band more or less can change the world.

"Is your band any good?" he asked Gary.

"Yeah, I think so. Right now, we're doing a lot of

covers, but we're trying to develop our own sound." He stopped when the stranger began shaking his head sadly.

"You won't. Not unless you commit. Not until music becomes your reason for being, when it pervades every waking moment of your life, when everything you see and hear and touch and do becomes inextricably tied to your music."

Juliet stared at him in annoyance. What business did he have giving advice like that? And why was Gary listening so eagerly to him, taking it all in as if this total stranger possessed some special, secret knowledge of life?

"I'd like to hear your band," he said. "What's it called?"

"Incarnation." Gary smiled sheepishly. "Yeah, I know it's kind of pretentious . . ."

"It's only pretentious if you can't live up to it."

"We've got a gig in a couple of weeks, at Barney's Grill. It's a dive, but it gets a good crowd. Maybe you could come, see what you think of us. We'll probably practice later on tonight, here. It might be boring for you, but—"

"It might not."

Gary was beaming, as though he'd just been praised for his potential by some renowned professional—not some guy off the street who was claiming to have amnesia. Juliet's annoyance was becoming a tight knot in her stomach. She wished Keith would come. She turned as footsteps approached. But it was only Bill Dean, the Gamma president, and his latest girlfriend, Darcy something.

Bill greeted the stranger warmly. "Hey, how's it going? Remember anything?"

"Nothing at all."

"This is so wild," Darcy bubbled. "Bill told me about you. I mean, you could be *anybody*."

"Or nobody," he replied.

"Are you doing anything to help yourself?" Juliet asked sharply. "Have you seen a doctor?"

"I feel fine," he said.

"Then go to the police," she said. "See if there's a report on a missing person who fits your description."

"I think a person has to be missing for 72 hours before the police will take a report," Bill said.

The stranger rose. "I won't impose on you that long."

"Where are you going?" Gary asked anxiously.

"There must be a shelter or something in the Loop where I can stay for a while."

"That's not necessary," Bill said. "We've got plenty of room here. Stick around."

Juliet watched the stranger carefully. He didn't seem terribly surprised by Bill's offer, nor did he appear wildly grateful. He nodded, as if he'd expected the invitation. "All right. Maybe I can do something to earn my keep. Shovel snow, wash cars . . ."

"We'll work something out," Bill said.

Darcy was eyeing the stranger coyly. "It must feel so strange, having amnesia. Like you were born yesterday."

Gary sounded almost envious as he added,

"You've got no history, no past. Nothing to tie you down."

He acknowledged this with that odd half-smile. "I don't even have a name."

"We have to call you something," Bill said. "Got any names you like?"

He shrugged.

Darcy clapped her hands. "Ooh, what fun! We'll pick a name for you!"

Juliet remembered what she had in her bag. She pulled out the baby name book.

"Great," Bill said. He leaned over Juliet's chair as she flipped through the pages. "What do you want, a common, ordinary name? Or something unusual?"

"Which do you think would suit me, Juliet?" he asked.

"I haven't the slightest idea," she replied briskly. "Let's see . . . according to this, the most common name for boys in the United States is Michael."

"No good," Bill said. "We've already got three Michaels living here now."

"Okay, here are other popular names," Juliet said. "David, Andrew, James . . . do any of those appeal to you?"

"Oh, let's not give him an ordinary name," Darcy whined. "He needs something exotic. Mysterious." She was practically batting her eyelashes at him.

"Exotic," Juliet repeated. "How about a name from Shakespeare?" She read aloud from the book, selecting only the most bizarre ones. "Balthazar, Cornelius, Horatio . . . "

41

"Romeo?" Gary suggested. "No, Keith might not appreciate that."

Juliet shot him a look, and returned to her book. "There are listings of French names, Irish names . . . what about something from the Bible? Matthew, Mark, Luke, John," she prattled, and then stopped suddenly.

"You like that one," he said.

"John? It's all right."

"No, before that. Luke."

Juliet swallowed. "Not particularly."

"*I* like it," Darcy announced. "I think it's sexy."

"And we don't have any other Lukes in the house," Gary said.

"How does it sound to you?" Bill asked the stranger. "Do you feel like a Luke?"

Juliet tried to ignore the prickly sensation on the back of her neck. She forced herself to look at the boy. This time, at least, he wasn't looking at her. He was gazing upward, studying the ceiling, with that damned half-smile, as if he found all this discussion remarkably amusing but was too polite to laugh.

"Yes," he said. "I think I do."

"Then Luke it is," Bill proclaimed.

The book slid off Juliet's lap and fell on the floor. She picked it up and shoved it back in her bag. "Excuse me," she murmured, and hurried out.

42

CHAPTER · 4

Juliet sat on Keith's bed and waited while he fiddled around with his computer.

"I just want to enter this data before I forget," he murmured.

He'd arrived at Gamma house just as dinner was about to be served, so they hadn't had a chance to speak privately at all. Juliet tapped her foot restlessly as she watched him hit the keyboard.

"There, I'm done," he announced, looking up. Then he said, "Is everything all right?"

"Sure, why do you ask?"

"You don't look very happy. I thought you might be mad at me for being so late."

Juliet brushed that aside. "It's okay."

"Something's bothering you." He joined her on the bed. "You barely said a word at dinner."

"It's no big deal," Juliet said. "Well, maybe the conversation bothered me, the way everyone's acting so goofy about that guy, like he's so special . . ."

"He *is*, in a way. How many amnesiacs have you ever met? It's interesting. The guy didn't exist before last night."

"Of course he existed," Juliet retorted. "And he's probably some very ordinary guy, who goes to school or has some ordinary, boring job. Dani thinks this whole amnesia thing is a scam."

"Dani," Keith repeated. "Not exactly the world's most down-to-earth person. She hasn't even met him."

"Even so," Juliet persisted, "how do we know if this guy's legitimate? He hasn't even been to see a doctor."

"We shouldn't call him 'this guy' anymore," Keith mused. "He's got a name now."

"Luke," Juliet said.

"Bill says you named him."

"I just recited names. *He* picked it." She looked at him quizzically. "Don't you think it's strange that he picked *that* name?"

"Why?"

"Because he looks so much like Luke Dennison."

His brow furrowed, then quickly cleared. "Oh, yeah, the rock star. Well, it's also the name of a few thousand other people, Jules."

"I guess," she admitted grudgingly.

"The guys like him. Gary thinks he's terrific."

Juliet sniffed. "Of course he likes him. Did Gary tell you that the guy—Luke—is trying to talk him out of going to law school?"

"Gary's got a mind of his own. He's been having second thoughts about law school for awhile." He draped an arm loosely around Juliet's shoulders. "I think you've just decided you're not going to like

44

Luke, and you're looking for a way to rationalize your feelings."

As always, he made sense. "I guess you're right."

"What I can't figure out," he went on, "is *why* you've taken such a dislike to him."

"I don't know," Juliet admitted. "There's just something about him . . . oh, forget it. Let's go to the movies."

Downstairs they heard the strains of music coming from the basement. "Gary and his band are practicing," Keith said. "Want to go down and listen for a minute? We've got time."

"Sure." Juliet had heard them practicing before, but she'd never paid much attention. Now she was curious to find out what Gary was thinking of throwing away a career in law for.

They went down to the basement where about half a dozen Gammas and some girls lounged around on beat-up sofas. Luke was there, too. The four band members were playing at one end of the room.

Juliet and Keith sank down on one of the sofas. Kyle, the drummer, finished off the tune with an energetic solo. There was a smattering of applause.

Gary, on lead guitar, didn't look happy. "Where the hell's Danny?"

Michael, on bass, replied. "I think he went out."

Gary frowned. "This is the third practice in a row he's missed. I say we start looking for another singer."

There was a general rumble of agreement from the other band members. "We've got a gig in less

45

than two weeks," the keyboard player, Josh, reminded them. "We'd better find one fast."

Gary ran his fingers through his hair. "Let's run through 'Cold Flame.'"

Josh began pounding out a rhythmic opening run on the keyboards that sounded familiar to Juliet. It obviously was familiar to someone else, too.

Luke stood up. "I know that song."

Josh stopped playing. Luke ambled over to the podium.

"Can you sing?" Gary asked.

"I don't know." Luke nodded toward Josh, who started the introduction again. Kyle picked up the beat, and Gary and Michael followed.

Luke began to sing. *In the chill of the night, through the bite of the wind, can you feel the heat . . .*

Juliet sat upright. She did know that song, she'd been listening to it just the night before. It was an old Luke Dennison song.

And this Luke *could* sing. His voice was deep, strong, with a raspy rough edge. The lyrics were subtle but sensual, suggesting a physical exchange between two people that kept them warm. As he sang, Juliet could almost feel the heat, the chill. Not just because of the words.

Because he sounded like Luke Dennison.

She looked around to see if anyone else had noticed this. Keith was nodding his head in time to the music, and smiling appreciatively. Everyone was listening with interest, but no one seemed to share her reaction. Maybe they hadn't listened to Luke Dennison in a long time. Or maybe this was all just her imagination.

No, that was impossible. As Dani often told her, she had no imagination.

Luke didn't move much while he sang, but his body seemed taut, tense, as if he were straining against an impulse to move. Then, as the song reached its climax, he closed his eyes and arched his body backwards. His voice jackknifed through the still room.

In the chill of the night, through the bite of the wind, I melt in the heat of your flame.

As Gary's last chord faded away, there was an utter silence in the room. Then one of the boys whistled, and Darcy let out a squeal.

The guys in the band were clearly impressed. "You can sing," Michael said.

Gary was staring at Luke with unconcealed admiration. "That's an understatement. You sang that just like Luke Dennison."

Juliet was relieved. So she wasn't just imagining it.

Darcy sidled over to her. "He's sexy, don't you think?"

"If you like the type," Juliet replied.

"Who wouldn't?" Darcy giggled. "Those jeans . . ."

Juliet gave a noncommittal shrug. But the snug jeans were sexy, she had to admit.

The band started up again, this time playing an old Eagles tune. "You know this one?" Gary called to Luke.

"No." He strolled away and returned to his seat. Someone offered him a cigarette, and he accepted. The band fumbled for awhile, with Gary providing a feeble vocal rendition of the song. After a verse, his voice trailed off, and he waved for the band to stop.

"You want to learn this?" he asked Luke.

"Why?" Luke asked.

"You could join us. I can't promise much in the way of money, but we split what we get. We could start hustling, try to get some regular work."

Luke took a drag off his cigarette and blew out a stream of smoke. It was impossible to tell if he was seriously considering the offer.

"You've got to do something, right?" Gary continued. "At least, until you recover your memory and find out what you've been doing for a living."

"You guys ever do original stuff?" Luke asked.

"I've written some music," Gary said. "None of us are very good at lyrics. Can you write?"

"Don't know. I can take a shot at it."

"You're a natural performer," Darcy piped up. "Hey, maybe this is what you were before, a singer with a band."

"Maybe," Luke said. He stubbed out his cigarette. "It doesn't matter though, does it? It's what I am now."

Juliet rose. "Keith, let's go." She started out of the room and went up the stairs, not even looking to see if he was following her. She hurried to the closet and retrieved her coat. Keith came up behind her.

"It's too late to make the movie," he said.

"Then let's go somewhere and get coffee, or something," she replied. "I don't feel like hanging around here."

"What did you think of the band?" he asked in the car. "Not bad, huh?"

"Something strange is going on," Juliet blurted out. "This guy shows up looking like Luke Dennison. He takes the same name. He gets up with the band and he sings like Luke Dennison. And you're all acting like this is totally normal. Am I the only person who thinks this is just a little weird?"

Keith stopped at a light and gave her a quizzical look. "What are you saying? You think he's a reincarnation of Luke Dennison or something like that?"

She couldn't help laughing at the mild alarm in his voice. "Of course not. What I think is that this is all some sort of carefully calculated scheme. There are just too many coincidences going on here. And if it's not a scheme, well, it *is* spooky."

Keith drove in silence for a moment. Watching him, Juliet could almost see his mind working, processing the data and searching for the solution.

He spoke slowly and deliberately. "I think there's a perfectly rational explanation. Here's my theory. Luke, or whatever his real name is, was a big Luke Dennison fan. There are still plenty of them around, right? Maybe he was one of the fanatics, the kind who collected pictures and old concert ticket stubs. The ones who think he was some kind

49

of god."

"Or the ones who think he's still alive, hanging out with Elvis," Juliet said.

"Exactly. And people have always told him he looks a little like Luke Dennison, so that encourages his interest. Can you accept this as a possibility?"

Grudgingly, she nodded.

"Okay," Keith said. "Now, let's take this a step further. This guy suffers some kind of head injury, and he has amnesia. He needs an identity. You say the name 'Luke,' he recognizes it, he finds it appealing. If Luke Dennison was such a powerful influence on him, he had to know all the songs by heart, so well that they transcend the memory loss. And when he sings, he automatically imitates Luke Dennison."

His explanation was so logical that Juliet felt foolish. "You're right. Let's forget about him, okay? Tell me how your project's coming along."

"I think it's going to happen," he said. "But I'd better warn you, it's a lot of work. I'm going to be pretty tied up with it for the next few weeks. If I want to get this thing funded, I have to come up with a pretty comprehensive proposal. So if I seem a little distracted or neglectful . . ."

"It's okay," she told him. "I understand."

"Thanks for being so sensible. Some girls throw a fit if their boyfriends don't call every night, or show up late."

"I'm not that kind of girl."

"I know." He took his eyes off the road just long

enough to give her an appreciative smile. "That's one of the things I love about you."

It had started to snow. They were on the Drive, where they'd picked up Luke the night before. The wind from Lake Michigan blew the snow around, making it seem heavier than it really was. Juliet looked out the window and shivered.

"Cold?" Keith asked. "I'll turn up the heat."

In the chill of the night, through the bite of the wind, can you feel the heat . . .

"What are you humming?"

"Huh? Oh, that song the band was playing. Now I can't get it out of my head."

"I hate when that happens," Keith commented. "Damn!" The car alongside them skidded slightly, and Juliet gasped. But Keith swiftly turned the wheel, expertly maneuvering the car to avoid an accident.

Keith exhaled. "It's okay. You all right?"

She could feel her heart racing. "That was close."

"Don't worry," Keith said. "You're safe with me."

"I know," Juliet replied.

CHAPTER · 5

"**Y**ou haven't seen Keith in *how* many days?" Dani leaned against her locker and gaped.

"Ten." Juliet twirled the combination on her own locker and opened it.

"So what's going on? Is the great romance of the century fading?"

"No." She exchanged one textbook for another and pulled out her coat. "He's working on a big project. I called you Saturday night, to see if you wanted to go to the movies, but your mother said you were out." She let the last words hang in the air, as a question.

Dani flushed slightly. "Remember that blind date I had last weekend?"

Juliet looked at her with interest. "You mean, he didn't turn out to be a computer nerd after all?"

Dani busied herself with the zipper on her jacket. "He's okay. I wouldn't exactly call him the man of my dreams, but at least if I go out with him occasionally, it will get my mother off my back." She put her hands on her hips, pursed her lips, and went into a pretty credible impersonation.

"You're only interested in gangsters and hoodlums. Why can't you go out with a nice boy? Why can't you be like Juliet?" She punctuated this by giving Juliet an exaggerated scowl of accusation.

"I can't help it if I'm a paragon of virtue," Juliet replied. "What's his name, your nice boy?"

"Joel. He's taking me to a basketball game at De Paul tonight." There was a noticeable lack of enthusiasm in her tone. Then she brightened. "Want to come with us?"

"No, thanks. I'm actually seeing *my* nice boy tonight. A famous anthropologist is giving a lecture at Northwestern this afternoon, and we're having dinner afterward." They started down the hall toward the exit. "Why would you want me coming along anyway? Don't you want to be alone with him?"

"Alone? At a basketball game?" They went outside, and Dani paused to tie her scarf tighter around her neck. "To tell the truth, I wouldn't care if we were going on a moonlight walk by the lake, you could still come along. It's not like I'm madly in love with him."

"That's such an odd expression," Juliet mused. "'Madly in love.' Like there's supposed to be an element of insanity in a relationship."

"There *should* be. I'll know when I'm really in love, because I'll feel crazy, desperate, wild with desire, utterly miserable when I'm not with him." She glanced at Juliet. "Don't you feel that way

53

about Keith? How can you go ten days without seeing him? Aren't you madly in love?"

"I love Keith," Juliet responded promptly. "But I've got my own life, too. I don't have to be with him every minute of the day."

"But you *want* to be with him, don't you?"

"Of course I do. I'm happy when I'm with him, we're comfortable together. He makes me feel good."

"Good." Dani snorted. "Don't you want to feel more than good and comfortable? Don't you want rapture, passion, reckless abandonment?"

Juliet laughed. "That's movie love, Dani."

"Well, it's what I want," Dani said stubbornly. "And I don't get those feelings from Joel."

"Give the poor guy a chance," Juliet urged. "Keith and I were seeing each other for two months before we realized how right we were for each other. You've known Joel less than two weeks. Maybe he'll grow on you."

"He's not going to grow into Luke Dennison," Dani said mournfully. "Speaking of which, what ever happened to that guy with amnesia?"

"Don't know, Keith hasn't mentioned him."

"I guess I was wrong about him being a con artist," Dani mused. "He's been there at Gamma house—how long?"

"Two weeks."

"And he hasn't run off with all the brothers' worldly goods, right? So what's he doing, mooching off of them?"

"He's doing odd jobs around the frat house in

exchange for room and board. Listen, I've got to run. I want to get some homework done before I go up to Northwestern."

She didn't have all that much homework, it was just an excuse to cut off the conversation. She'd never been a very good liar.

It was unusual that she hadn't kept Dani up-to-date on the amnesiac. Dani didn't know the guy's name was now Luke, and she didn't know he was singing with Incarnation.

Why was she keeping this from her, she wondered. What was she afraid of?

She finally came up with an answer for herself. She didn't want Dani to get hurt, and that's why she'd been unwilling to talk too much about Luke. He was just the kind of guy who would appeal to her, with her romantic notions of love. She was afraid that Dani would insist on meeting him, fall madly in love, and be devastated when the guy recovered his memory and took off. Now that she'd rationalized her behavior, she felt better. As always, she was just watching out for Dani's best interests.

It occurred to Juliet that it would be nice to have her own car that evening. Keith had been working so hard that he was bound to be tired, and she didn't want to make him take her home. So when she cut through the university quadrangle, she decided to stop at her father's office and see if the car was available. She entered the building that housed the English department and climbed two flights of stairs.

55

Her father's door was ajar. "Dad?"

He looked up from the pile of papers on his desk. "Juliet! What a nice surprise. Come on in."

"I hope I'm not disturbing you."

"Not at all."

"I just came by to ask if I could take the car. I'm going to a lecture up at Northwestern, with Keith."

"Yes, of course, my dear, take the car."

"I'll be careful driving," she added.

"Oh, I'm not worried," her father said. "You're a better driver than I am." He leaned back in his chair and studied her thoughtfully. "But then, you've always been a very sensible girl. I've often wondered where you get that from." He chuckled. "Not from me, certainly. And your mother, ah, she was a romantic."

"In what way?" Juliet asked curiously. Her father hardly ever spoke of her mother.

"Impulsive. Spontaneous. I remember her waking me up once at three in the morning to come outside and look at the moon." Memory made his eyes hazy. "I read poetry to her. Shelley and Keats, as I recall. She could hear a poem once or twice and recite it back to me by heart. And she loved music. I think she knew the words to every love song ever written."

Juliet wanted to know more. She had so few memories of her mother, and these moments of intimacy with her father were rare. But then her eye was caught by the clock on his desk. If she wanted time to get home, do her homework, shower, and change, she'd have to get moving.

She told him so, and he nodded abstractly. "Yes, yes, of course. Have a nice evening."

She hurried home, and managed to keep to her schedule, timing her departure so she wouldn't hit the rush hour traffic. As a result, she reached Gamma house a half hour early, and she knew Keith probably wouldn't be back there yet.

She debated a walk around the campus, but the sidewalks were slushy, and she was wearing nice shoes. She could sit in the car and wait, but that was silly. She'd hung around Gamma house alone before; why was she hesitating now?

She knew why. She didn't want to run into Luke. But this was silly of her, and she wasn't about to let him have an impact on her life this way. Resolutely, she left the car and went to the door. The boy who opened it confirmed that Keith wasn't back yet, invited her to make herself comfortable in the living room, and disappeared.

She sat down and picked up the newspaper lying on a table. But she'd already read it that morning, so when she heard footsteps approaching, she quickly looked up, eager for a distraction.

She stiffened when she saw who was standing there. "Hello," she said coolly.

"Hi," Luke said. "I haven't seen you around here for awhile."

She nodded, without bothering to offer an explanation. "How are you?"

He bowed his head solemnly, and imitated her formal tone. "Very well, thank you. And you?"

"Fine."

He looked well. He was wearing black jeans, and they looked new. It occurred to her that in every photo she'd ever seen of Luke Dennison, he was wearing black. Recalling Keith's explanation, she decided this Luke's attire was appropriate—he was doing everything possible to emulate his hero.

He'd had his dark hair trimmed. It was still long, but not so scraggly. Jeans and haircuts cost money, she thought.

He must have read her mind. "I've discovered I have some carpentry talent. I've been able to make some money building bookshelves for the guys here. So you don't have to worry that I'm mooching off the fraternity boys."

She flushed. "I didn't say you were."

"You were thinking it."

She wasn't about to give him the satisfaction of admitting that, so she changed the subject. "Are you still practicing with Incarnation?"

"We're writing some new songs." He indicated a notebook in his hand. "I've been working on lyrics for Gary's music. Would you like to see something I've written?"

He extended the notebook, as if he assumed her answer would be yes. For this very reason, she was tempted to say no. But that would be so rude. And as Keith had pointed out, she really didn't have any logical reason for disliking Luke.

She took the notebook, which he had opened for her. She planned simply to scan the page, and hand it back with a polite "very nice."

But words, phrases, leaped off the page and

demanded her attention.

> *Caught in a cataclysm of our own making,*
> *We are blind to the lightning,*
> *The thunder is silent . . .*
> *Look for meaning in the chaos, if you choose,*
> *You have nothing to lose,*
> *But your mind.*

It went on for two pages in the same mode. As she read, she actually became caught up in the images, confusing as they were. They had unnerving implications. It didn't make for pleasant reading.

Her expression must have reflected this, because Luke said, "You don't like it."

"What is it about, exactly?"

"Exactly?"

She looked up. Was he mocking her? It was impossible to tell.

He took his time before responding. "Oh, seeking truth, making sense of emotional confusion. Life. Or maybe death. What do you think it means?"

Life, death . . . how pretentious, she thought. He was trying to impress her. He wanted her to be awed, dazzled. She wasn't going to give him the satisfaction of knowing she *did* find the lyrics . . . well, mildly intriguing.

She handed back the notebook. "It doesn't read like a song. It's more like a poem, isn't it?"

"That's what songs should be. Poems set to music."

"But doesn't a song need rhythm? This is so . . ." She struggled for the right word, not too harsh, but something to demonstrate how unimpressed she was.

He came up with the word first. "Messy?"

How was it he could so easily turn one word into a challenge? She nodded defiantly. "Yes. It's messy."

He wasn't offended. "Life is a messy business." He stated that as if it were an absolute truth, and his presumption irritated her.

"I don't believe that," she said. "Life *can* be messy, but it doesn't have to be. You just have to exert some control. You make goals, and you make plans to reach those goals."

He smiled. "Who was it who said that life is what happens when you're making other plans?"

She had no idea. Nor did she understand why everything he said seemed to antagonize her. "What are you saying? Don't make goals, don't have plans, just . . . *be*?"

"Something like that. Goals are just setups for failure. How many plans actually work out?"

She rose. That didn't put them at eye level, but at least it brought her closer. "Is that why you talked Gary out of going to law school? Because it was a goal?"

"Gary only *thought* he wanted to go to law school. It was his father's idea. He was doing it to make his father happy." He gave a short laugh.

"There's nothing wrong in trying to please your parents," Juliet shot back.

"What's the point in that?"

60

"To make them happy!" He was baiting her, and she struck back. "But I guess you can't understand that, since you don't have any memory of your parents, do you?"

"No, I don't," he replied, his smile widening. "I'm a lucky guy, aren't I?"

She was appalled. "You think that's good, that you don't remember your parents?"

"Maybe we all need to develop amnesia," he said. "So we can start living for ourselves, not for our parents. So we can do what we want to do, not what we're expected to do. Think about it, Juliet. So much of the way people behave is based on their past, their parents, their old relationships and failures. So much of what a person does with his life is based on guilt or some self-imposed sense of responsibility. The past turns into emotional baggage that we drag around for all our lives. It weighs us down."

His words were dizzying. In some crazy way, they almost made sense. She took a step backward, in an attempt to regain her mental balance, to give herself some distance so she could formulate a response.

"Doesn't it bother you that somewhere out there your mother and father, maybe brothers and sisters and friends, are worried sick about you?" Her voice rose with every word. And even as she spoke, she wondered why she was getting so worked up. This wasn't any business of hers.

He wasn't getting worked up. "Personally, I think I'm better off not knowing. Do you know what amnesia has given me, Juliet? Freedom."

"Freedom," Juliet scoffed. "Freedom to do what?"

"Freedom to invent myself."

She wanted to jeer, but all she could manage was a nervous, unsteady laugh. "You mean, turn yourself into a bogus Luke Dennison?"

He didn't respond. And suddenly, she wished she hadn't said that. Her hostility was washed away by a wave of inexplicable sadness. Or was it fear? How strange, how disconcerting, not to be able to recognize one's own emotions. Those eyes, those damned eyes . . . they were trying to tell her something. Or ask her something. Or they were probing her, trying to identify the feelings she couldn't name. She wanted to blink, to turn away, but she couldn't.

She didn't know how long they stood there like that. And then the front door opened.

"Jules, I'm sorry!"

She tore her eyes from Luke's. "What? Oh, Keith, hi! What are you sorry for?"

"I was talking to this professor, and I couldn't walk out on him. I know how much you wanted to hear that lecture, and I feel like a real heel about this."

Gradually, his words penetrated and started making sense. She actually had forgotten all about the lecture. She looked at her watch as Keith explained to Luke, "We had plans to go hear this famous anthropologist, but it's too late."

62

"Plans," Luke echoed. "I enjoyed talking with you, Juliet. I hope I'll see you again soon."

Juliet nodded mutely, and Luke left the room.

"Gee, Jules, I can't tell you how sorry I am about this." Keith looked truly repentant, and Juliet had no difficulty forgiving him.

"It's okay. I know how hard you're working."

He was clearly relieved. "I'll make it up to you. How about going out for sushi?"

"You hate sushi," Juliet reminded him.

"But you love it. And this can be my concession for making you miss the lecture."

Juliet had to laugh. "Raw fish as a penance. That's silly, Keith. Let's go to that Mexican restaurant."

"What were you and Luke talking about?" Keith asked as they walked out.

"The band. The new songs he's writing. I read some of the lyrics."

"Oh, yeah? What did you think of them?"

All she could say was "Weird."

"They're playing this weekend at Barney's," Keith said. "I'd sort of like to hear them. I know that probably doesn't appeal to you . . ."

She slid into her seat and adjusted the seat belt. As he got in the other side of the car, she looked out the window, hiding her face from him.

"Actually," she said. "I wouldn't mind."

CHAPTER · 6

During the last school period on Friday, Juliet's class was shown a documentary video about space exploration. Like practically everyone else in the room, Juliet was slumped in her seat, observing the program through half-closed eyes. This particular teacher had been showing them videos every Friday afternoon since they'd returned from the Christmas break. Like the seniors, this teacher was coasting, killing time till graduation.

Juliet had already seen this particular documentary in another class, and it hadn't been all that interesting the first time. So when a folded note was passed to her she snatched it up gratefully.

The note was from Dani, who sat two rows ahead of her in the next aisle. "What are you and Keith doing tonight? Whatever it is, can Joel and I do it with you?"

She could hear Dani's plaintive voice in the request. She read the note again, hoping—in vain—that the words might change before her very eyes. Then she made the mistake of looking up. Dani had turned around in her seat, and Juliet was confronted with beseeching eyes. Juliet nodded briefly, and she was rewarded with a happy smile.

Well, she couldn't keep Luke a secret from Dani forever. She was bound to find out about him sooner or later, especially if Luke continued singing with the band. At least if Dani was with Joel, she mused, she couldn't go too nuts over Luke.

She felt reasonably certain Dani would be attracted to him, though. Juliet had to acknowledge that he had a charismatic quality. Maybe that was why his face kept popping into her head. She recalled their last conversation at Gamma house and involuntarily shivered. She was glad she herself had enough sense not to be susceptible to his strange charm.

Actually, it could be fun tonight, she decided. She was curious to see how the band had shaped up. Dani's date, Joel, was probably an okay guy, despite Dani's lack of enthusiasm for him. And having another couple with them might improve the conversation. At least it would discourage Keith from talking about his project.

The final bell rang before the documentary was over. Nobody cared. Juliet joined Dani at the door.

"Thanks for letting us hang out with you guys tonight," Dani said. "Joel and I are running out of things to talk about."

"After only two weeks?"

"I don't think we're on the same wavelength. He talks about politics and the stock market. I want to talk about . . . "

"What?"

Dani gestured vaguely. "Life. We're just very different."

"Well, they say opposites attract," Juliet remarked. "Of course, I've never really believed that. I think a couple needs to have things in common if they want a relationship to last."

"Such as?"

"Interests. Goals . . . "

They stopped at their side by side lockers. As Juliet busied herself with her combination, Dani turned and called out to someone. Greetings floated back.

"Who was that?" Juliet asked, not looking.

"Amy and Heather." Dani opened her locker. "It's funny. You remember how we used to all hang out together? It just hit me that I have no idea what's going on in their lives. School's not even over yet, and already we're drifting apart."

"It happens," Juliet replied. "We're all getting ready to move on. We're changing."

"You haven't changed," Dani pointed out.

"You want me to change?" Juliet asked, grinning.

"Are you crazy? I depend on you. You're the only person I know who has two feet permanently attached to solid ground."

Juliet shook her head in amusement. Just a short while ago Dani was criticizing her for being too staid and predictable. Now these same qualities were virtues. That was Dani for you. Jumpy and erratic and full of contradictions. Which was why she needed someone down-to-earth, like Juliet, to watch over her.

"Where are we going tonight?" Dani asked as they left the building.

"Barney's. Incarnation is playing."

"Those guys from Gamma house?" Dani made a face. "Remember when they played at the Spring Dance last year?"

"They've improved since then," Juliet said. She hesitated. Was this the time to tell Dani about the new singer? No, she'd just start speculating and fantasizing and she'd get herself all worked up.

"What are you wearing?" Dani asked.

"I don't know," Juliet said. "Jeans, I guess."

"Let's walk by Lulu's and check out the windows," Dani suggested. "I wouldn't mind something new to wear. Okay?"

"Sure, why not?" Juliet said. They turned and strolled down to 53d Street, the main shopping drag in the area. It was lined with take-out food places, funky little boutiques, and used bookstores, including the one Juliet worked in on Saturdays. Tucked between a small grocery and a Laundromat was one of the funkiest of the boutiques, Lulu's.

"Ooh, I like that," Dani crooned. The headless mannequin in the window wore a thin, practically transparent baby-doll dress.

"You'd freeze," Juliet commented.

Dani groaned. "Jules, do you have to be practical *all* the time?"

"I thought you wanted me to be dependable," Juliet protested, laughing as she opened the door.

As always, Lulu's was a carnival of color and sound. Madonna was blasting through the store, and Madonna wannabees were searching the racks. In Juliet's opinion, Lulu's was too trendy, with its MTV attitude and racks of dresses giving you the choice of looking like a tramp or a waif. Dani took off to examine the baby-doll dresses.

Juliet went to a rack and began flipping through the clothes without much interest. But as she pushed hangers aside, a dress caught her eye.

Maybe it was the vibrant, jewellike blend of colors that grabbed her attention. She pulled the dress off the rack and looked it over.

It wasn't her style at all. She'd always worn classic clothes, tailored and fitted. This was a flowing dress, made of some silky material—it had a gypsy look about it. Exotic.

Dani returned, without any clothes in hand. "Those dresses make me look like I'm twelve years old," she complained.

Juliet held her dress out at arm's length. "What do you think of this?"

"Pretty," Dani said promptly. "But I can't wear that green. It turns my skin yellow."

"No, I mean for me." She turned away so she wouldn't have to see the surprise on Dani's face. "I'm going to try it on."

When she emerged from the dressing room, Dani was just outside by the mirror. Juliet turned around. "How does it look?" Having seen herself in the dressing room mirror, she already knew the answer.

"Wow. I've never seen you in anything like that. Jules, you look *hot*."

Juliet accepted the compliment graciously, but that wasn't the word she would have used. She thought she looked like a cross between a flower child and a model for a Pre-Raphaelite painting. Neither were images she'd ever thought to cultivate.

"It's not really me," she murmured, but as she whirled around in front of the mirror, she felt almost giddy. A fleeting image crossed her mind— the fantasy Juliet, the one she saw when she listened to old Luke Dennison albums.

The dress might not be her style, but she thought she looked prettier than usual. It struck her that her smile seemed brighter, her eyes had a different sparkle . . . of course, the hair was all wrong. With a dress like this, she couldn't wear this prim headband that held her shoulder-length hair neatly in place. If she washed it and let it dry naturally, without using a blow dryer, it would curl a bit and have a wild, untamed look . . . In her mind, she envisioned herself dancing in this dress. But for some reason the man she imagined herself dancing with wasn't Keith. It was some faceless stranger.

She realized Dani was looking at her oddly. "What are you thinking about?" Dani asked.

"I might buy it."

Dani slapped the side of her own head. "I can't believe it! Juliet Turner is buying a dress that makes her look sexy!"

"You mean, I'm actually being unpredictable?"

Juliet teased. She took another look at herself. "Oh, I don't know. It's not me."

"Of course it's not you. But what's wrong with doing something out of character once in a while?"

"It's a little . . . outrageous."

"Then get it," Dani exhorted her. "If you can't act wild and crazy, at least you can look it." She checked the price tag hanging from the sleeve. "It's on sale."

She wanted this dress. She couldn't remember ever wanting a dress so much. Before she could change her mind, Juliet changed back into her own clothes, took the dress to the counter, and paid for it.

"Keith is going to flip when he sees you in this," Dani noted.

"I doubt it. He never pays attention to how I look."

They parted, with plans to meet at Juliet's at eight o'clock.

When she got home, the new housekeeper, Mrs. Dixon, was vacuuming the hall. She greeted Juliet, and noticed the bag in her hand.

"You've been shopping."

"Yes."

The housekeeper smiled encouragingly. Juliet could tell she was expecting to be shown the purchase. In normal circumstances, Juliet would have. But she'd only hired this woman less than a week ago, the housekeeper didn't know her well, and this dress might give the wrong impression. So

70

she just smiled in the friendliest possible way and murmured something about being in a hurry.

Up in her room, she took the dress from the bag, put it on a hanger, and hung it in her closet. Next to her other clothes, it looked odd and out of place. It seemed to be saying "go wild and crazy, dance till dawn." What kind of girl wore a dress like this? she asked herself. A girl who was reckless and unpredictable, a girl who would dance till dawn, with . . . no, not Keith. With someone like Luke Dennison. Or someone who looked like him.

Again, for the second time that day, a shiver ran through her. She was beginning to wonder if she'd ever have the guts to wear the dress when the phone rang.

"Hello?"

"Hi, Jules, it's me."

"Oh, Keith, I'm glad you called. I wanted to warn you. I told Dani she and her new boyfriend could come to Barney's with us tonight. You don't mind, do you?"

When there was no immediate response, she went on. "Look, I know you think Dani's nuts, and if you really don't want them to come—"

"It's not that."

His voice was low, and his words were followed by a sigh, so she knew what was coming.

"Juliet, don't hate me for this. But there's a guy in town, some major big-shot from M.I.T. I've been invited to a dinner my professor's having for him. Jules, I've got to meet this guy—he's one of the most important people in my field." His words were coming out in a rush, like he was afraid he'd lose his nerve if he didn't get them out fast.

"I know, it's the second time in a week I've done this to you, and I'm really truly sorry . . ."

"I know, I know." Juliet sighed. She had to be practical and not let Keith's announcement bother her. She was too mature to fuss and wail when she knew this was important for his future.

"You could still go, with Dani and her friend."

"No, it's okay," she said. "I'll wait till you can go. I'm sure the band will be playing there again."

They ended the conversation on the same note, both trying to smooth things over, and made a date for the following night.

Still, after hanging up the phone, she experienced a wave of annoyance. She fought it off by reminding herself that this was the kind of relationship she'd chosen, the kind she'd been happy with for a year. She and Keith had their own interests, their own lives beyond each other. It was a sensible relationship. Maybe it wasn't wildly romantic, but she knew she would never have one moment of pain with Keith.

She kept her hand on the phone. She'd call Dani now and tell her they wouldn't be going to Barney's after all, that she and Joel were on their own. She dialed, but the line was busy. I'll call her later and cancel, she told herself.

But for some reason, she never got around to doing that.

* * *

72

There was nothing particularly remarkable about Barney's Grill. It was a smallish place with wobbly wooden tables and uncomfortable chairs, a limited menu of greasy food, and absolutely no decor or ambience. It smelled of spilled beer and stale cigarette smoke, and there wasn't any space for dancing.

But it was always packed, for several reasons. It featured live music. It was cheap, with a two-dollar cover charge. It was conveniently located just north of the Loop, so it drew students from both the north and south sides of town. Most importantly, patrons' ID's were rarely checked. So for about five dollars, a person could have a couple of beers and listen to local bands that just might be halfway decent. They rarely were, but one could always hope.

The clientele of Barney's dressed every which way, from punk to preppie, so Juliet knew her gypsy dress wouldn't look peculiar. Even so, she had the sensation of being in a costume as she walked into the noisy club with Dani and Joel. She felt not-quite-herself.

"Aren't you freezing?" Dani asked as they took off their coats. The heating system at Barney's wasn't terribly effective.

"Not really," Juliet replied. Joel had moved ahead of them in search of a table, so she took the opportunity to whisper, "I like him. He's seems like a nice guy."

"Exactly," Dani muttered, her tone making it clear that she didn't put much value on that quality.

Juliet privately agreed that Joel wasn't a terribly vibrant person to be around. But he was pleasant, and nice-looking. He didn't act dismayed when he discovered that Juliet would be joining them. He even made a feeble joke about what a lucky guy he was to have two dates.

At that moment, having located a vacant table, he was beckoning to them. The girls moved toward him. As they sat down, Dani put her elbows on the table. It tipped precariously, almost knocking over a half-filled beer mug that had been left there. Joel caught it just before it spilled onto Dani. Dani didn't bother to thank him. She wasn't even looking at him.

A waitress ambled over to take their orders. Juliet ordered a light beer, and Dani asked for tequila. Joel only wanted a soda. "I'm the designated driver," he told the waitress. Juliet smiled her approval at him. Dani only rolled her eyes.

"Make that *two* tequilas," she said to the girl. Her eyes were searching the room, restlessly. Rudely, Juliet thought. She herself noted a number of Keith's fraternity brothers in the dimly lit room, but she didn't want to leave the table to greet them. She had to compensate for Dani's inattentiveness.

She smiled brightly at Joel. "Do you come here often?"

"Not very much. Too noisy. Who's playing tonight?"

"Incarnation," Juliet told him. "They're from Northwestern."

"Oh, yeah, I've heard them," Joel said. "They do a lot of oldies, right?"

"Not so much, anymore," Juliet replied. "They've got a new singer." She glanced at Dani, who was still gazing around the room. She raised her voice slightly as she told Joel the story of Luke.

Sure enough, this got Dani's attention. "He's a singer? The guy who looks like Luke Dennison? Why didn't you *tell* me?" She was practically bouncing in her seat. "Is he any good? What's his name?"

Joel seemed taken aback by her sudden enthusiasm, and Juliet couldn't blame him. He'd probably never seen Dani so excited.

The waitress appeared with their drinks. Dani downed a tequila with one gulp and ordered two more. In an undertone, Juliet warned, "You're going to get drunk."

"So what? *I'm* not driving. Tell me about the singer." But Juliet didn't have to. Barney, the club owner, was at the microphone on the small stage. The short, plump man didn't wait for any reduction in the noise level, and Juliet could just barely make out his words.

"Welcome to Barney's," he said in a laconic voice. "We're pleased to present Incarnation."

It wasn't much of an introduction, and there was only a scattering of applause. The regulars at Barney's rarely had high expectations of the bands. The lights were low on the stage as shadowy figures took their positions.

When the lights came up, Kyle was behind the

drums, Josh stood at the keyboards, Gary and Michael were poised with their guitars on either side of the stage. Luke was up there, too, in front of the other guys, but with his back to the audience. It wasn't until Gary played some opening chords that Luke whipped around and received the full benefit of the spotlight.

"Ohmygod," Dani breathed. She grabbed Juliet's arm. "He *does* look like Luke Dennison."

Maybe it was just a combination of the odd lighting and the cigarette smoke, but Luke seemed to have a glow around him, an almost surreal bluish haze. He clutched the microphone, but he didn't take it off the stand. Instead, he lowered his head slightly and pulled himself toward the mike. He began to sing.

> *I could tell you I don't want you,*
> *I could tell you good-bye,*
> *I could say I never cared,*
> *And it might not be a lie,*
> *But we can't break the chains . . .*

It was a simple song but a dark one, telling of a couple who wanted to break free of each other but were unable to because of their mutual dependence. It was charged with mixed emotions, recriminations. And Luke's voice, his expression, communicated the confusion and tension unequivocally.

Juliet was vaguely aware of the room growing quiet, and of a pain in her arm where Dani was digging in with her fingernails. The song ended with a moan, a futile plea for freedom, a cry of despair that reverberated through the room long after the music stopped.

Luke didn't acknowledge the applause that followed. He signaled the band to go directly into the next number. This one was pure rock and roll, with a hard, driving beat. The lyrics weren't subtle. The song was an explosion, an outburst of intense feeling and desire for some woman.

Juliet tore her eyes away from Luke to glance at Joel. He seemed to be enjoying the music, nodding his head in time to the drum beat. Then she looked at Dani, and her friend's expression triggered a faint warning bell.

Dani's face was drained of color, and her eyes were glazed over. As the song ended, Juliet leaned past Joel and spoke to her. "He sounds a lot like Luke Dennison, doesn't he?" she asked casually. "And he's calling himself Luke, too. Funny coincidence, huh?"

Dani didn't respond at all. The waitress reappeared with two more tequilas, and Dani drank silently.

Song after song, Luke had the room mesmerized. Even though Juliet had heard Luke sing in practice with the band, she wasn't prepared for this. In the fast, hard-driving songs, Luke didn't bellow or shout—he raged. When he sang a love song, there was no crooning, no artificial sentiment. Each word became a physical caress.

It was hard to believe Luke alone had written all these songs in the short time he'd been working with Incarnation, but Juliet knew he had. She barely knew him, yet she realized that each song had his mark on it, some quality that told her none of the other guys had written the words.

At one point, she thought Luke was looking directly at her. But she couldn't be sure. She was so oblivious to everyone else in the room, she could have been imagining that. And why would he be looking at her, anyway?

Maybe he was looking at Dani. She turned to her friend. Dani was shaking, her breathing was shallow.

Alarmed, Juliet asked, "Are you okay?"

Joel, too, was staring at Dani with trepidation.

"It's Luke," Dani whispered.

"He's *like* Luke," Juliet began carefully, but at that moment waves of applause drowned her out. This usually blasé audience was going berserk, not just with clapping but with masculine whistles and hoots, feminine screams.

While Josh, Gary, Kyle, and Michael grinned and took bows, Luke simply left the stage and disappeared behind it. Dani pushed back her chair.

"Where are you going?" Joel asked.

Dani didn't answer him. Juliet rose and went after her. Joel got up, too.

They followed her behind the stage to a tiny storage–dressing room. Luke was there, sitting on a bench, his head in his hands. He looked up when they all entered.

Dani's words came out in a breathy whisper. "I know you."

Juliet gaped. "You mean, you know who he is?

78

You've seen him before?"

Luke's gaze was impassive as Dani rushed forward. "Luke. You *are* Luke. I always knew you weren't dead; you couldn't be."

With horror, Juliet realized what Dani was really saying. She put a hand on Dani's shoulder and tried to keep her own voice steady. "Dani, honey, you've had too much to drink. You know he's not really Luke Dennison. Even if Luke Dennison isn't dead, he'd be much older than this guy is."

"He *is* Luke, he is," Dani insisted wildly. "I've been waiting for so long, and now I can feel it. He has the magic—no one else in the world could have that magic."

Joel just stood there, looking helpless and confused and distinctly embarrassed. Juliet waited with apprehension for Luke's reaction. Would he mock her? Would he sneer?

Tears were streaming down Dani's face. Luke stood and hovered over her. Very gently, he put his hands on her shoulders. His voice was low.

"What are you waiting for, Dani?"

"You." She strained toward him, her body taut and tense, but Luke held her at arm's length.

"No, not me." He touched her face with a finger, tracing a tear as it made its way down her cheek. The gesture seemed to calm her a bit. He continued to speak, softly, soothingly. "You're waiting to find some meaning for your life, Dani. You want something to believe in."

"I believe in you," Dani whispered.

"Look inward, Dani. Find the magic in yourself.

79

It's there, inside you."

All the tension in Dani seemed to dissolve. Her body went limp.

Joel stepped forward and spoke to Juliet. "Maybe I should take her to the car."

"That's a good idea," Juliet murmured. Dani didn't protest as Joel took her arm and led her away. But as they neared the door, she looked back. "You *are* Luke Dennison," she charged.

"I'll be right there," Juliet called after them. Then she turned to Luke. "Thank you."

"For what?"

"For being kind to her. She . . . she's got a lot of problems. Feelings that have been building up inside her."

"Everyone has feelings," Luke said. "She just lets hers show."

"Mmm. Well, I'd better go. . . ."

"Don't worry about Dani," Luke told her. "She'll be all right. She's on a journey of discovery, just like we all are. Do you understand what she's searching for, Juliet?"

Dumbly, she shook her head.

"She said it herself. Magic. She thinks it's in the music. But music . . . it's just a guide, you know. Like a signpost on a road. I'll bet you want to find magic, too, Juliet. But all your goals and plans and schedules . . . they get in the way, don't they."

His words washed over her, making sense and not making sense. Her brain ordered her feet to step backward, but she took a step forward. She could feel his breath now.

"It frightens you, Juliet. The magic. It's a risk, and you like to be in control. You're afraid of what you'll find if you let yourself search for it. But you have nothing to fear. Celebrate the magic, Juliet. Embrace it."

His hands were on her shoulders now. And then he was kissing her. In her mind, she knew what she should do: pull free, push him away. But she did nothing, nothing at all. Never before in her life had she felt so unable to exert her will.

And then it hit her—why she'd had such a strong negative reaction to him at first. She'd been fighting her own attraction to him.

Far away, music was playing. It was a record, a currently favored song, a sentimental ballad. The corny lyrics permeated the dense fog in her head— *I know it's wrong, but it feels so right.* Now she understood why songs like that became so popular.

She also heard the sound of approaching voices, the other boys in the band. That provided the impetus to pull free.

"They're waiting for me," she said. "Dani and Joel. I have to go." She couldn't look at him, she didn't dare. She ran from the room.

No one spoke much in the car on the way home. Dani stared out the window. In the backseat, Juliet did the same. Of course, she couldn't see anything in the pitch-black darkness. But in a way, that was appropriate.

Joel was driving fast. He obviously couldn't wait to get rid of both of them. He dropped Juliet off first.

"Thanks, Joel. Dani, I'll call you tomorrow." Only the briefest of nods told her that Dani had heard her.

Up in her bedroom, she undressed, got into bed, and prayed that sleep, blessed unconsciousness, would come very quickly and rescue her from her dangerous thoughts. But sleep could be perilous, too. Who knew what she might find in her dreams?

CHAPTER · 7

When she woke the next morning, Juliet's first thought was thank goodness she'd be working at the bookstore all day. A typical Saturday there was busy, and she'd have no time to remember, to reflect on the night before.

She rolled over in bed to look at the clock on her nightstand. But first her eyes settled on a small, framed photo, a snapshot of herself and Keith that Dani had taken the previous August. They were sitting on a rock overlooking Lake Michigan, and Keith had his arm loosely draped over her shoulder.

She forcibly moved her eyes to the clock. It was only eight o'clock. She had two hours to kill before she had to be at work.

Showering and getting dressed didn't take up even a quarter of that time. She decided to surprise her father with a big breakfast. In the kitchen she examined the contents of the cupboards and the refrigerator and discovered some pancake batter mix and maple syrup. She busied herself mixing the batter, and then she set the table.

She was about to heat up the skillet on the stove burner when it dawned on her that her father should be awake and downstairs by now. She went out to the foot of the stairs. "Dad? You up?"

There was no response. She ran upstairs and knocked on the closed bedroom door. Then she looked in.

Her father's bedroom was empty. She frowned. She knew her father's routine as well as her own, and there was no place he could have gone this early on a Saturday morning. Then she realized that his bed hadn't even been slept in.

Panic seized her. "Dad?" she called out loudly. She was just starting back down the stairs when she heard the sound of a key in the front-door lock.

"Dad! Where have you been?"

He gave her the oddest smile, proud and abashed at the same time. "Well, I had a date last night..."

"A date?" In connection with her father, the word sounded foreign.

"Yes. She's a new member of the faculty. Psychology."

"What's she like? Where did you meet her?"

"At the Cranstons' retirement party last week. She lives next door to them." As he took off his coat, Juliet noticed that he wasn't wearing a tie. Her father must have realized this at the same time, because he touched his collar. "I must have left my tie at her place." Now he looked really embarrassed.

Juliet grinned at him. "Tell me about her."

"She's very interested in the psychological interpretations of the Romantic poets. Of course, that's not consistent with my own neo-Aristotelian approach—".

"Dad! C'mon, I'm making us a nice breakfast, and I want to hear all about her. *Not* her research."

Over pancakes and strawberries, she interrogated her father. Ultimately she was able to ascertain that the woman in question was named Eleanor Wrightson, that she was in her forties, and that she was smart and pretty and had a sense of humor.

"I'd like you to meet her sometime," her father said. "If you wouldn't mind."

"Mind? I'd be delighted!" She gazed at him fondly. Over the years, colleagues had tried to fix him up with women, but it had never come to anything. Despite his devotion to his work, he had to be lonely sometimes. Even though she'd continue living at home after graduation, she'd be busy with school, her job, friends . . . and Keith, of course. She liked the idea of her father having a companion.

Her father did the cleaning up after breakfast, and she took off. She made it to Brooks Books just as Fran Brooks was raising the bars in front of the store. Juliet waved at her and went in.

The tall, slender owner of the store greeted her, looking harried. "Oh, am I glad to have you here today! I had five deliveries this week, and I haven't even had a chance to open the boxes. By the time those books get on the shelf, they'll be off the best-seller lists."

85

"No problem," Juliet told her cheerfully. "I'll get it all done."

Fran eyed her thoughtfully. "Something's different about you. Are you wearing makeup?"

"No."

"I guess it's just being in love," Fran said. "How *is* Keith?"

"He's fine." Juliet's cheeks began to burn, and she turned away. "I'll get started on those boxes."

Brooks Books was an eclectic shop. Fran carried the usual commercially successful books, but she also bought used books on every conceivable subject. The place was popular with students, since Fran paid top dollar for their old books and resold them relatively cheaply. Between unpacking books, putting on price stickers, shelving the books, and helping customers, Juliet was kept happily busy all morning.

After lunch, things became a little more quiet. Fran was assisting the sole customer and Juliet was at the cash register when Dani came in.

"Dani! I was going to call you this afternoon." Juliet searched her friend's face. "Are you . . . how are you feeling?"

"I'm okay." Dani smiled slightly. "Listen, I'm sorry about last night. I must have made an awful ass of myself."

Juliet offered her an excuse. "Tequila can be lethal."

Dani nodded. "Tequila, on top of the way I've been feeling lately . . . and then listening to Luke." She winced. "Totally freaked me out."

"He was nice to you about it, though."

"Yeah, sure, but I don't know, there's something strange about him."

"That's an understatement," Juliet remarked. "He has amnesia and he looks and sounds like Luke Dennison. Yes, I'd definitely call that strange."

"It's not just that," Dani mused. "I mean, it *is*, but it's more. He's . . ." She fumbled in search of a word. "He's scary. I don't mean like a psycho serial killer. It's the way he sees things. His songs . . . am I making any sense at all?"

An image of Luke passed through Juliet's mind. She could feel the hair on her arms rise. "Yeah. I guess he is a little scary."

"I'm sure he thinks *I'm* nuts," Dani said. "If you see him again, apologize for me, okay?"

The phone rang, and Juliet picked it up. "Brooks Books."

"Hi, Jules, how're you doing?"

Keith's voice shot waves of guilt through her. The feelings were intensified by his tone—so tentative, like he was afraid she was still holding a grudge about the night before.

She put extra warmth into her response. "I'm fine, how was the dinner last night?"

"Good. The guy from M.I.T. acted like he was really interested in the project. But I'll tell you more about it later. I heard the band was great last night. Luke said you were there."

Juliet's stomach turned over. What else had Luke told him?

"Yeah, they were good."

"They're playing again tonight, and I'd like to hear them. Would you want to go again?"

Now her stomach was doing somersaults. "Gee . . . I don't know."

"Or we could do something else. Whatever you want to do."

Juliet gripped the phone tightly. It was a shock, a chilling perception, to realize that what she wanted to do was to see Luke again.

"Jules? Are you there?"

"Yes, yes, I'm here."

"What do you want to do?"

Juliet began carefully. "I don't mind going to Barney's." She looked at Dani, who was leafing through a book on the counter. "Maybe Dani could come with us, too. The band really was awfully good, worth hearing again."

Dani's head jerked up. She shook her head in an almost violent manner.

"No, never mind," Juliet said. "It can be just us."

"Whatever you want," Keith said. "Should I pick you up?"

"No, I'll meet you there. Around eight, okay?"

She hung up the phone and met Dani's curious gaze. "Why in the world would you want me tagging along with you and Keith?"

"Why not? You let me come with you and Joel last night."

"That's different. I'm not in love with Joel."

"You sure you don't want to come?" Juliet asked.

"No. I'm sorry, Jules, but . . ." She made a helpless gesture. "I just can't handle hearing that

88

music again. Not yet. I've got to go. Talk to you later."

Juliet put her elbows on the counter and rested her chin in her hands. Why had she wanted so much to have Dani with them tonight? She explored a variety of answers. Because she wanted Dani to deal with whatever had upset her so much last night. Because it might keep Keith from talking about his research.

Or maybe because she wanted as many friends as possible around her tonight. She needed all the protection she could get.

Protection—from what? It wasn't as if she expected Luke to assault her. She could easily avoid being alone with him. With a growing sense of something like panic, she acknowledged that she didn't need protection from Luke.

She had to be protected from herself.

* * *

She didn't even think to ask her father if the car would be available that evening. It wasn't until she was ready to leave for Barney's that she learned he needed the car himself.

"I'm taking Eleanor to a restaurant on the north side," he told Juliet. "We can drop you off on the way. Will you be able to get home?"

Juliet assured him that Keith would drive her home. While she waited for her father, she took a moment to examine her reflection in her bedroom mirror. The plain brown sweater with jeans tucked into scuffed cowboy boots were in marked contrast to the way she'd looked the night before. She'd dressed down on purpose. It was another form of protection.

She left with her father, and they drove a short distance. He pulled up in front of a large, rather grand three-story house. "This is where she lives?" Juliet asked in awe.

"It's quite a place, isn't it?" her father. "Come see the inside."

Juliet's first impression of Eleanor Wrightson was a pleasant surprise. She didn't know what she had expected, but it certainly hadn't been this petite, curly-haired, youthful woman with laughing eyes.

"I'm so glad to meet you, Juliet," she said, exuding sincere warmth.

"I'm happy to meet you, too," Juliet replied promptly. She looked around at the spacious foyer, and the wide, winding staircase. "This is a lovely house, Ms. Wrightson. I mean, Dr. Wrightson."

She placed a hand lightly on Juliet's arm. "It's Eleanor. I grew up here. Now that my parents have retired to Florida, it's all mine." She looked around. "It's way too big for me, really. I should rent out the third-floor rooms to young people. If you know of anyone looking for a place, let me know. I wouldn't charge too much."

As she spoke, Juliet couldn't help noticing her father's expression. He was gazing at Eleanor with a look she'd never seen on his face before. He was positively aglow, beaming with pride and happiness. Why, he's in love, Juliet thought.

They all chatted pleasantly on the way to Barney's, but when they arrived at the shabby club, Eleanor looked at Juliet with concern. "You don't mind going in this place alone?"

"It's okay," Juliet said. "I'm meeting my boyfriend inside."

"You don't have to worry about Juliet," her father said. "She's very self-reliant and independent. Always in control of the situation."

Juliet nodded in confirmation. But as she got out of the car, she wondered how well her father really knew her. Lately, she wasn't very sure how well she knew herself.

If Barney's had been crowded the night before, it was packed tonight. Word must have spread fast about the new Incarnation, and Juliet had to scan a sea of faces and push through the mob in search of Keith.

"Juliet!"

She turned and saw one of the Gammas, Jake Kingsley, sitting at a table with his girlfriend, Lauren something. Juliet waved politely and turned to move on, but Jake was beckoning her over.

"Keith's going to be late," Jake reported. "He got caught up in some work. Sit down with us."

Juliet smiled thinly. She had no desire to spend the evening with this couple she barely knew, but there didn't seem to be any vacant tables in the place. She took one of the two empty seats at the table.

After a little small talk, Jake and Lauren

basically ignored her and returned to their private conversation. Juliet managed to flag down a waitress and order a soda. Then she stared at the door, waiting for Keith to show up.

She couldn't help overhearing Jake and Lauren. "It's a great band, I've been listening to their practice sessions," Jake was telling Lauren. "They've got this new singer . . . hey, there he is now."

Juliet was grateful that her soda appeared at that moment. It gave her something to focus on. She made a concerted effort not to look in the direction that her table mates were looking.

But once again, she had that eerie sensation of *feeling* his presence. The sensation was borne out a second later.

Jake jumped up to greet Luke and introduce him to Lauren. Juliet drained her soda. Then she heard the other vacant chair scrape along the floor. Luke was sitting next to her.

"Juliet."

She moved her head slightly. "Hello, Luke."

"It was nice of you to come again."

Was he thinking she had come just to see him again? She wanted to dispel that notion immediately. "Keith heard how good the band was and he wanted to hear you," she babbled. "He'll be here any minute."

"I'm glad you're here," he said simply.

She knew she should probably say thank you, but the words were stuck in her throat.

Luke went on. "There's a new song. I've been working on it for awhile, but it needed something.

An inspiration. I finished it last night."

"Luke!" The call came from Gary. "Come on, let's get going."

He left the table. Now Lauren and Jake were looking at her with interest. "What was he talking to you about?" Lauren asked.

"I have no idea," Juliet replied. "When did Keith say he'd get here?"

Jake didn't know. The band members took their positions on the stage. Unlike the previous night, they were greeted with real applause. The audience was giving them its complete attention.

The audience wasn't disappointed. Incarnation was as exciting—as captivating—as they'd been the night before.

Juliet tried to relax and enjoy the music. But all the time, she was waiting. And she wasn't looking at the door.

The song came about halfway through the set. There was a sudden change of mood on the stage. Kyle set down his drumsticks, and Josh moved back from the keyboards. Only Gary strummed softly as Luke sang.

> *I know something,*
> *that you can be,*
> *A part of me,*
> *I've engraved you on my heart,*
> *Like a hidden tattoo . . .*

It wasn't a typical love song. In fact, the word love was never spoken. It was all yearning and urgent need, and as he sang, Juliet was aware of her whole body shuddering, straining. It was as if invisible strings were attached to her, trying to pull her toward him, and it was only the force of gravity that kept her in her chair.

When the song was over, the band took a break. Juliet sank back in her seat, exhausted.

"Gee, Keith's missing a good show," Lauren commented. "That guy, Luke, he's fantastic."

"Yeah, he could start a whole new fad," Jake said.

"What do you mean?" Juliet asked.

"Well, you know, like all those Elvis impersonators running around. He could be the first Luke Dennison impersonator."

Juliet responded quickly. "Don't call him an impersonator. He's not a mimic. Those are completely original songs."

She didn't realize how fierce she sounded until Jake held up his hands in a mock show of defense. "Hey, back off! What are you, the president of his fan club?"

"Don't be silly," Juliet snapped. She wished they'd go away.

They read her mind. Seconds later, Lauren took off for the ladies' room, and Jake ambled to another table to talk with friends. She was alone.

But not for long. "Did you like my new song, Juliet?"

"Yes."

"I hope it didn't embarrass you."

She could fake a look of innocence, bewilderment, pretend she had no idea what he was talking about. But she did know. And she knew that he knew.

He sat down. "Barney has asked us to do a regular gig here. Every Friday and Saturday night."

"That's nice."

"Yeah. I can afford to find a place of my own now. Do you know a room somewhere I can rent?"

"I might."

"Near you?"

She raised her head, and looked directly into his eyes, the eyes that had pierced her, frightened her. Now, they seemed to her to be like windows. She could see beyond them. And she wasn't scared.

"Yes. Near me."

Then, beyond him, she saw Keith. He was standing in the doorway, and he was watching them. Even from this distance, she could make out the puzzled, uneasy look on his face.

He's worried, she thought. And with a new clarity, a sort of melancholy thrill of comprehension, she finally acknowledged to herself that he had a very good reason to be.

CHAPTER · 8

Under normal circumstances, it only took Juliet one cup of coffee to wake herself up in the morning. But on Sunday morning, she was already on her third cup, and her head hadn't cleared at all. She was no closer to sorting out the jumble of images and sounds that cluttered her mind than she'd been when she tossed and turned in bed the night before. She was still reeling from her own perceptions.

There was one image she wished she could erase altogether— Keith, in the car, driving her home. On the surface, everything seemed normal. They talked about the music and some of the people they'd seen at Barney's. But every time they stopped at a light, he turned to her, his eyes filled with unasked questions. And she had no answers for him.

Her father came into the kitchen. "Good morning, my dear."

"Would you like me to fix you some breakfast, Dad?"

"No thanks, I'll just have some coffee. Eleanor and I are going out to brunch."

Juliet picked up on the subject of Eleanor eagerly. She wanted to know more about their relationship, and not only because she cared about her father. It might get her mind off her own situation.

"You and Eleanor are getting pretty serious, aren't you, Dad?"

Her father seemed slightly unnerved by the question. "What makes you think that?"

Juliet smiled. "Oh, for crying out loud, Dad, you're spending enough time with her."

He almost blushed. "Well, I *am* very fond of her."

"More than fond," Juliet interjected.

He gazed at her worriedly. "Does that bother you, Juliet?"

"Of course not! Dad, I'm happy for you. Someday, I'll be leaving home, and I wouldn't want you to be alone. You need someone to . . . to . . ."

"Take care of me?" her father suggested with a twinkle in his eye.

Juliet smiled. "Well, you aren't exactly the most down-to- earth person in the world."

Her father patted her arm. "You've done an excellent job of taking care of me, Juliet."

Juliet laughed. "Dad, I promise I won't be jealous if Eleanor wants to take over that job."

"Did you have a pleasant evening?" her father asked.

"Yes, very nice," she replied automatically. "How was yours?"

97

"Marvelous." He joined her at the kitchen table with his cup of coffee.

"Good restaurant?"

"Yes, I suppose it was. I can't say that I paid that much attention to the food." A flustered grin flickered across his face. He sipped some coffee to regain his composure, and then, in a too-casual voice, he asked, "What do you think of Eleanor?"

"She seems very nice. I liked her."

"Good! She liked you too."

The joy in his response brought the first smile of the morning to Juliet's face. "You know what, Dad? I think you're in love."

Her father considered this. "Maybe I am. I know that I haven't felt this way since your mother . . ."

Juliet leaned forward and interrupted. "How do you feel, Dad?"

"I don't know how to describe it." He paused thoughtfully. "Isn't this interesting. I'm a professor of poetry, and love must be the favorite topic of poets. Yet the only word I can come up with is . . . dizzy!"

Juliet nodded. "It's a good word. Dad . . ."

"Hmm?"

"Are you *madly* in love with her?"

It was a silly question. The mere idea of her mild-mannered father in a state of romantic insanity was absurd. Yet she wasn't really surprised when he nodded slowly.

"You know, dear . . . I think perhaps I am."

Madly in love . . . She remembered how she'd mocked Dani for using that phrase. Now, hearing them again, the words didn't sound quite so bizarre anymore.

"Madly in love," her father repeated slowly, savoring the words. "Yes, it's a good description." He looked at her with interest. "Would you say you're madly in love with Keith?"

Juliet never thought she would use a corny expression like 'saved by the bell,' but that was what she was thinking when the doorbell echoed through the house.

"I'll get it," she said quickly, but he rose, too, and followed her to the front door.

"Eleanor! I was going to pick you up."

"I decided to walk," the woman said. "Hello, Juliet. Isn't it lovely out? The snow is melting. You can smell spring in the air."

Juliet leaned out and gave an appreciative sniff. "You know, you're right."

"Spring," her father mused. "The favorite season of poets."

"I can't wait to start gardening," Eleanor said. "I've already picked up seeds."

"Gardening," Mr. Turner repeated. "I'd like to try that this year."

Juliet was floored. Her father had never shown any interest in gardening before. Their own backyard was a maze of weeds and overgrown grass. It was remarkable how being in love could change a person.

"Of course, spring also means mowing lawns," Eleanor noted. "I'm not looking forward to that. Maybe if I rent one of my spare rooms, I could reduce the rent in exchange for some chores like that."

"Are you serious about renting a room?" Juliet asked. "Because I may know someone who would be interested."

"Keith?" her father asked.

"No, someone else. I might be speaking to him today."

Eleanor fished around in her purse. "I have an extra key here. Why don't you take it, and then you can bring your friend by the house anytime today to show him the room."

Juliet was surprised. The woman hardly knew her, yet she was trusting her with the key to her home. The surprise must have shown on her face.

"Your father's always talking about how mature and responsible you are," Eleanor said. "The room's the one at the end of the hall on the third floor."

"Thanks," Juliet said, taking the key. "I'll get this back to you later."

"Actually, you can just give it to your father." A slight flush rose on her face. It was matched by the color of her father's face.

Juliet realized Eleanor was anxiously awaiting her reaction to that. She smiled and affected nonchalance as she stuck the key in her pocket. "Fine. Have a nice brunch."

"Would you like to join us?" her father asked.

"No thanks. I've got things to do."

After waving them off, she returned to the kitchen, washed up the coffee cups, and willed the telephone to ring. When it actually did, she could feel her heart rate accelerate. Calm down, she scolded herself. It could be Dani. Or Keith. Or a total stranger offering a deal on a magazine subscription.

But it wasn't.

"Hello, Juliet."

"Luke! Oh, I'm so glad you called." Then, to cover up for what might have sounded like overreaction, she switched to a businesslike tone and offered an excuse for her enthusiasm. "You see, I was just talking to this friend of my father's, and she has a room to rent out in her house. I've got the key. Do you want to look at it today?"

He did. She gave him directions by public transportation to her own house, hung up the phone, and spent the next hour straightening up. She glanced periodically out the front window, and when she saw him coming round the corner, she slipped into her coat and met him outside.

She barely gave him a chance to greet her and kept up a constant stream of inconsequential chatter. "We can walk from here, it's not far. It's a nice neighborhood, don't you think? Most of the people who live around here are connected to the university, but some people just like Hyde Park because it's like a small town in the middle of a big city."

She was blabbering, and she knew it. She couldn't help herself. Just being by his side was so unnerving. She couldn't even put a name to the jumble of emotions that cluttered her head. Her only reaction was to keep on prattling, in the hope that she could keep these unfamiliar feelings from showing on her face.

Luke nodded, and smiled, and murmured "Uh-huh." Then, when she finally paused, he took a deep breath. "It smells like spring."

"That's what my father's friend, Eleanor, said. Do you remember spring?"

"I know it exists," Luke said. "I know it's supposed to smell like this. But it's like something I read, not something I remember ever actually experiencing."

"I can't imagine what it would be like to have amnesia. For you, everything is a new experience. You have no memories. And you don't seem to care."

"How can I care? I like not having memories. When you have memories, everything you experience is compared to something you experienced before. I can see everything for itself, for what it is. Look at that tree."

"What about it?" Juliet asked.

"Maybe I've passed that tree a million times," Luke said. "But I have no memory of that. So I'm seeing it for the very first time. It's new and interesting."

She watched his eyes as he spoke. Why had she never before noticed the incredible sweetness in them?

"You can see everything like a child," she remarked.

"Exactly. Everything is exciting. Frightening,

too. Everywhere I look, I see a sort of terrifying beauty."

She understood what he was saying. "Everything's a risk."

"Exactly. Children take risks, because they don't know any better. When people grow up, they stop taking risks, because they know the consequences of their actions."

"Like touching a hot stove?"

"Like falling in love."

That word . . . she looked at him sharply. Surely, he wasn't referring to them.

"There's the house," she said quickly. She walked ahead of him and unlocked the front door. And she hurried up the long, winding staircase. "The room is on the third floor.

"It's a little chilly," she said as they went down the third-floor hallway. "She's probably got the heat turned down up here, since she's not using this floor." She opened the door to the room at the end of the hall.

It was a big room with simple furnishings. "It looks bare," she commented.

"It's got everything I need," Luke said. He touched the plain maple desk. "I can write here."

"How do you write your songs, without any memories to base them on?"

"I write about what I see and hear right now. What I'm feeling. Right now. You feel it, too, Juliet."

"There's a draft, coming from that window . . ." she murmured. She turned away from him and faced the window.

He laughed, a deep, warm laugh. "Juliet . . ." His hands were on her shoulders. "Don't tell me you can't feel it."

She'd never been a good liar. There was no point in trying to lie now. "I feel it. But . . ."

"But what?"

"Keith." She brushed his hands away and turned to face him. "I love him. I *do*."

"I know that," he replied calmly. "But you're not *in* love with him, are you? Not madly in love."

That phrase again! She stared at him stupidly.

"Love is a kind of madness, Juliet. It's not something sensible and safe and predictable." His hands were back on her shoulders. She didn't push them away. "Don't be afraid to love me. Take the risk. Don't compare this to what you've felt before or worry about what you think might happen."

Her voice trembled. "What could happen?"

"I don't know," he said simply, honestly. "All I know is what I'm feeling right now. I love you."

"You love me," she repeated. "How can you say that? You don't even know me!" She wanted to protest more, but she had a feeling her words would be feeble.

"I know you," he said.

She shook her head, almost violently. "But you said yourself, you feel like you were just born. I'm the first woman you saw. A baby sees his mother, and he bonds to her, he loves her because she's the first person he sees. That's all I might be to you."

Slowly, his arms drew her closer. "Mother, sister, daughter," he murmured. "Lover. Everything."

She was in his arms now. And there was nothing more to protest about, because she was where she wanted to be.

They sank down onto the bed. And it was so easy, so effortless . . . they were connected in a way she'd never felt with anyone, ever before. There was no before, there was only now. She had no will, and she didn't care.

But even in her desire, in her sense of oneness with him, a spark of her sensible self remained. "No, Luke, it's too soon."

"I didn't know we had to follow a schedule."

She didn't want to leave his arms, but she forced herself. "I have to think. There are things I have to do . . ."

"Plans to make?" he teased.

Thank goodness there was a mirror over the dresser, and she could fix her disheveled hair and clothes. Through the mirror, she could see him, still lying on the bed. He was smiling, not angry at all by her sudden reluctance to continue. She smiled back.

"I can't change who I am," she said.

"I don't want you to change. I want you to be who you are. Who you *really* are, not who you think you're supposed to be."

Was it possible to feel nervous and happy at the same time? She had to stop trying to identify her emotions. With Luke, it would be impossible.

"We can't stay here. Eleanor might be back any minute."

Luke rose from the bed and followed her out.

105

"It's a beautiful house, isn't it?" she asked as they went down the stairs to the second floor. "Look at this banister. It's probably the original one."

He stroked the ornate, curved banister decoration on the landing. Then, without warning, he perched himself on it and slid all the way down to the first floor.

Juliet burst out laughing and ran down the stairs. "You are a child!"

They were still laughing when the front door opened. "Juliet, hi!" Eleanor exclaimed. "I'd forgotten you were showing the room." She laughed. "I guess I've got too many things on my mind."

Juliet's father appeared behind her.

"Dad, hi." It dawned on her that if they'd arrived only a few minutes earlier, their meeting with her and Luke might have been extremely awkward. But instead of distressing her, the image only made her giggle.

The same thought must have occurred to Luke, because he was laughing, too. Eleanor and Dr. Turner gazed at them in bewilderment.

Somehow, Juliet managed to make proper introductions. "Are you a student?" Eleanor asked.

"No, I'm with a band," Luke told her. "But don't worry, we won't be practicing here."

Fortunately, Eleanor didn't ask too many questions, probably assuming that since he was a friend of Juliet's, he had to be reasonably respectable. Luke, in turn, was courteous and agreeable, and Juliet could see that both Eleanor and her father were charmed by his pleasant, polite manner.

Rental terms were agreed on, and Luke told Eleanor he'd be moving in that afternoon. They refused Eleanor's offer of coffee and left the house.

They were quiet walking back. At some point along the way, she realized that they were holding hands. It seemed completely natural, totally right. Like they'd been together forever, like they'd be holding hands for the rest of their lives.

"Is there someone sitting on your front steps?" Luke asked.

There was. The shrubbery by the side of the door concealed the face, but she recognized the jacket. She slipped her hand out of Luke's before Keith saw them.

Keith rose as they approached. "Hi, Juliet. Luke." He didn't seem at all surprised to see them together, but Juliet rushed to offer an explanation anyway.

"Luke was interested in renting a room, and I was showing him a place . . ." Her voice trailed off.

"I better go pick up some stuff if I'm going to move in this afternoon," Luke said. "Thanks for your help, Juliet. See you, Keith."

Juliet watched him stride away. Then, aware of Keith watching her, she said, "Come on in. I wasn't expecting you. We didn't have a date today, did we?"

She couldn't look at him. She was afraid her face would give her away. Of course, she was going to have to tell him. But she needed time to prepare. It was going to be a shock for Keith. Probably as much as it had been for her.

What had happened in the past hour . . . it was as if a hurricane had swept through her world, her heart and soul. Emotions were colliding, changing, moving . . . nothing was the same anymore. She was dazed, elated . . . and totally bewildered.

"Give me your coat," she said as she took off her own.

"No, that's okay, I'm not staying long." His tone was distant, almost formal.

Busying herself with her coat and a hanger, she asked, "Is there a problem with your project?"

"No."

"What's bothering you?"

"Look at me, Juliet."

Reluctantly, she did. There was no anger in his face, just a sort of resigned sadness when he said, "I know there's something going on between you and Luke."

Should she deny it? she wondered wildly. Should she put him off, or make a joke, or hedge . . . No. Keith deserved better than that from her.

She began carefully. "There's . . . an attraction."

"No. It's more than that. I saw it last night, and I saw it just now. You've always been honest with me, Juliet. Don't stop now."

Her eyes welled up with tears. He was so good, so kind. "I don't want to hurt you," she said brokenly. "I don't know how it happened, I don't even know *what* happened. And whatever it is, I didn't mean for it to happen."

"I know," he said. He was in pain, she could see that, and she felt wretched.

"I'm so sorry, Keith."

"Don't worry about me. And don't feel guilty. You can't help what you feel."

She gazed at him in wonderment. "You don't care?"

"Of course I care," he said sharply. "I love you, Juliet. I'll always love you. But I'm being realistic. If you don't love me anymore—"

"But I do," Juliet broke in. "That's what's so—so confusing. Keith, I love you, but then Luke . . . yes, there's something I'm feeling, but I don't know what it is! It doesn't make sense!"

He took a moment to absorb this. When he spoke again, his voice was soft and sad. "Maybe you do love me. But I can see that you're in love with him, too. I have to accept that and get on with my life. I don't want to hold on to false hopes. I have to be—"

"Sensible," Juliet said. She hadn't meant for the word to come out as a criticism, but it did.

"That's the way I am," he said simply.

She nodded, ashamed. It had been a trait she'd loved about him. It was something she'd always felt they shared.

But everything was different now. And sensible—suddenly, that word didn't seem to have a place in her vocabulary.

"I still care about you," she began, but he put up a hand.

"It's okay, I know." He put a hand on the

doorknob. "Jules, I just want to say . . ." He paused uncertainly.

"What?"

"Be careful. Don't take too many risks."

Her head came up, her eyes widened.

"Whatever you're getting yourself into," Keith went on, "please take care of yourself. And if you ever need me . . ." The sentence went unfinished. She nodded. He left.

Whatever I'm getting myself into, she thought. She didn't know what that was. But whatever it was, it had . . . a terrifying beauty.

* * *

She was sitting at her desk that evening, halfheartedly completing an essay for school, when she heard the pebbles hit her window.

She went to the window and opened it. Luke stood on the ground below, looking up at her.

"What are you doing?" she asked.

"I just wanted to see you like that. I wish you had a balcony."

She had no problem this time identifying the emotion that surged through her. She smiled down at him. In a minute, she'd run downstairs and let him in.

But right that moment, she just wanted to take delight in feeling like Juliet.

110

CHAPTER · 9

Juliet opened her bedroom window as far as it would go and rejoiced in the warm breeze that greeted her. "It's really, truly spring."

She didn't realize that she'd spoken aloud until a voice behind her responded. "I should hope so. It's almost May."

Juliet whirled around. "Dani! I didn't hear the doorbell."

"Your father let me in. What was he doing with a shovel?"

Juliet grinned. "Gardening. Eleanor's got him working with her out back planting flowers. Can you believe it? My father, digging in the dirt?"

"Love makes people do crazy things," Dani commented.

"That's the understatement of the century." Her eyes went automatically to the frame on the nightstand by her bed. For a little over a month now, it had held a photo of Luke.

"Something's different in this room," Dani said.

"It's a mess," Juliet replied, with a rueful nod

toward the pile of clothes on the floor. "Remember how I used to keep this place spotless?"

But Dani was looking at the wall, at a square space where the paint was darker. "I know what's different. Your poster of Luke Dennison is gone."

"Yeah, I took it down."

"I can understand why," Dani said. "Who needs the fantasy when you've got the real thing?"

"I just thought it was juvenile," Juliet replied.

Dani picked up the open book on Juliet's bed and checked the title. "*Philosophic Dissent in Ancient Greece?*"

Juliet made a face. "It's on the reading list for a course I'm supposed to take this fall at the university."

"I've got something for you to read that's a lot more interesting." From her huge handbag, Dani withdrew the Sunday newspaper.

"The *Tribune*?"

"Third section, page forty-eight."

Juliet opened the paper and turned to that page. It was the entertainment section, and she immediately spotted the article Dani wanted her to see.

"Hot New Band in Town," the headline shrieked. She read aloud. "For over a month now, a little dive by the name of Barney's Grill has been featuring a band called Incarnation. This critic had the good fortune to stumble upon this joint last Saturday night, and I'm warning readers to catch Incarnation *now*. It won't be long before you'll be reduced to hearing them in some huge arena."

The article went on to rave about the music,

which it described as being "reminiscent of the best of the late sixties bands but with a driving, throbbing power that's all nineties. Incarnation consists of Gary Miller on lead guitar, Michael Lowenstein on bass, Josh Delacorte on keyboards, drummer Kyle Simpson, and singer Luke — who, interestingly enough, bears a striking resemblance to the late legendary Luke Dennison, both physically and musically."

She grimaced. "Why do they have to bring *that* up?"

"Kind of hard to ignore," Dani said. "Go on, read the last bit."

Juliet continued. "Luke goes by his first name alone. Perhaps the group anticipates that Luke, like Madonna, is going to be so big he won't need a last name. In my opinion, that's a pretty safe assumption."

She read those last two lines over again, to herself. "Wow, this is incredible!"

"You shouldn't be surprised," Dani remarked. "Hasn't Barney's been packed every night they play? That's what I heard."

"It's true," Juliet admitted. "Of course, I don't sit through every performance. Usually I wait for Luke in the back room."

"Why? Sick of the music?"

"Of course not," Juliet replied indignantly. "It's just that, well, this is going to sound silly. But there are these girls who call out to Luke and scream. They give me the creeps." Her lips curled in distaste. "Two of them have been showing up every

113

Saturday night wearing T-shirts that say 'Luke Dennison lives.'"

"You can't blame them," Dani said. "Remember how I reacted when I saw him?"

"That's different," Juliet replied. "You'd had too much to drink, and you got a little crazy, that's all."

"Yeah, okay, but you have to admit, it's pretty eerie. The way he looks, the way he sings, his name—come on, Jules, you were the first to say he reminded you of Luke Dennison."

"But I know him now, I love him, and I'm getting sick of the constant comparisons."

"Why?" Dani asked. "You used to adore Luke Dennison."

"Luke Dennison was a madman," Juliet said flatly. "He was a druggie and a drunk, and he burned out fast. *My* Luke—he's not like that. I wish people would just accept him for who he is."

"But who is he?" Dani said. "Has he ever figured that out?"

"No."

"What do you do for all that time backstage when the band's playing?"

"Like I said, I've got these reading lists from the university, so I bring books with me," Juliet told her. "I read backstage while they're playing, believe it or not."

That brought a smile to Dani's face. "*Not.* How can you get any reading done with all that music going on?"

"It's not easy to concentrate," Juliet admitted. "Not because of the music, though." She picked up the philosophy book and gazed at it regretfully. "I can't keep my mind on this stuff. It's funny, I was so excited about starting at the university. Now . . ." she shrugged. "I don't think about it at all. How could everything change so fast?"

"You're in love."

Juliet had no problem at all acknowledging that statement. "I was never like this with Keith. I want to be with Luke all the time. When I'm not with him, I'm thinking about him. Nothing else seems to matter . . ."

"I've noticed," Dani said dryly.

Juliet knew what she was implying, and she hung her head. "I'm sorry. I know I've been putting everything else in my life on a back burner. Including you, which is really lousy of me. You must hate me."

"Absolutely not," Dani replied. "And I'm not here to lay any guilt trip on you. I'm sure I'd be exactly the same way if I was madly in love." She perched herself on Juliet's bed. "So, the band's really doing great, huh?"

"Mmm. They have a manager now, some friend of Gary's, and he's been trying to contact record companies to hear them. And they're playing on Sunday afternoons now, as well as Friday and Saturday nights."

"You go to every performance just to sit backstage?" Dani asked.

"Luke likes me to be there," Juliet murmured. Then she gave Dani an abashed smile. "Can you believe this is me talking? Miss Independent, who

115

always said she'd never change her life for a guy?"

"Don't worry about it," Dani said. "Like I said, you're in love."

"In fact, I'm going over to Barney's now," Juliet said. "Want to come?"

"No, thanks. I've got a ton of applications to fill out."

"Applications for what?"

Dani fingered the fringe on the edge of Juliet's bedspread. "You know how I've been having some doubts about going to the University of Illinois this fall. Well, my father came up with this idea. He thinks I should spend a year in Europe. Paris, maybe, or Rome. Study a language, take some time to figure out what I really want to do with my life. So I'm applying to some schools there, and—why are you looking at me like that? Don't you think it's a good idea?"

Juliet was floored. In the past, Dani had done virtually nothing without consulting her. "You haven't mentioned a word about this to me!"

Dani replied matter-of-factly. "I haven't had ten minutes alone with you to discuss it."

Juliet closed her eyes. "Oh, Dani, you're right. I really am sorry. I feel awful."

"Don't," Dani said firmly. She reached out and clasped Juliet's hand. "It's time for me to start making my own decisions and standing on my own two feet." She paused. "I've been in therapy, you know."

"No," Juliet said. "I didn't know. Oh, Dani, I want to hear all about . . . *everything*."

116

"And I'll tell you all about it," Dani replied. "When you've got some time, give me a call."

"I'll make time," Juliet promised. They left the room together and started down the stairs.

"Will Barney's get a crowd this afternoon?" Dani asked.

"Probably. It was packed last Sunday."

"Don't you think it's strange," Dani mused. "All those people have come to hear the band, and no one's ever recognized Luke."

"Maybe he's not from around here."

"And he still hasn't been to see a doctor, has he?"

"Why should he? He doesn't feel sick."

"Hey, don't get defensive," Dani said. "Jules, he's got amnesia. That's not exactly healthy."

"I know," Juliet relented. "Look, I still think about it sometimes." She smiled. "Not when I'm with him, though. Then, nothing else seems to matter. He's absolutely fine just the way he is."

Dani smiled. "Who would have thought *you'd* be the one to go crazy over a guy who doesn't even have a last name?"

"Pretty weird, isn't it?" She paused at the front door. "Sometimes, I wonder if this is normal."

"Normal?"

"I don't feel like myself sometimes. Yesterday, I called in sick at the bookstore because Luke wanted to go on a picnic. I've never done anything like that before for a guy! I don't think about the future, about college . . . and the weirdest part is, I don't care! But my life is so wrapped up in his, and I don't know if that's healthy."

117

Dani groaned. "Give yourself a break, Jules! You don't have to be Ms. Independent Liberated Woman all the time. Besides, once you've been in this relationship for a while, things will settle down, you'll get into a routine, and you won't be so head over heels absorbed with him."

"How do you know so much about relationships?"

"I read a lot of romance novels," Dani replied promptly. They shared a laugh, like old times, and Dani took off.

Juliet ran to the kitchen and stuck her head out the back door. "I'm leaving," she called to her father and Eleanor. They both waved, but she doubted that they'd even heard her. Talk about two people absorbed with each other. It was reassuring to know she wasn't the only one.

But she couldn't imagine her feelings toward Luke ever becoming blasé, the way Dani had suggested. As she drove to Barney's, she tried to remember her life before Luke. It was as though she'd been only half a person. And she couldn't imagine a life without him.

Yes, she'd changed, and in wonderful ways. Luke had opened her eyes, he'd taught her how to let herself go, to appreciate things. She was learning to enjoy the moment instead of planning the next day. She could take pleasure in things she'd taken for granted—a beautiful day, the smell of a flower, the taste of a crisp apple. They could spend hours just walking, or reading poetry to each other, or listening to music.

And he was always telling her how important

she was in his life. She inspired his writing, he said. Once, when she asked him if he worried about not having discovered his true identity, he told her that she gave him all the identity he needed.

Sometimes, wrapped in his arms, she didn't know where she ended and Luke began. That oneness she'd experienced, the day they'd come together when she showed him the room at Eleanor's house—it hadn't faded at all. If anything, it had only grown stronger. Even when she was alone, she felt he was there, with her.

The band had already gone on by the time she arrived at Barney's. Every seat was occupied, and people were standing. Juliet slipped into the back room, sat down, and opened her book. The words of the ancient Greek philosophers danced before her eyes, refusing to make any sense or hold any appeal.

Her thoughts drifted back to Dani. She's getting her life together, Juliet thought. And that was great. But she wondered if she'd miss having Dani need her the way she used to. Then she considered her father . . . now that he had Eleanor, he wasn't so dependent on her, either.

Steve Lindsay, the band's manager, came in. "Juliet! I'm glad you're here."

She was startled by his tone of voice. He'd never seemed to show much interest in her presence before. The reason for Steve's unexpected congeniality soon became apparent. "I just had these photos of the band made up, and I want to send them with a tape to all the record companies.

119

You can address these labels, stick them on the wrappers, and stuff them."

Juliet was slightly annoyed by his imperious tone. "I've got some reading to do."

His tone switched to plaintive. "Hey, come on, I thought you cared what happened to this band."

I care about Luke, she wanted to say. But Luke was in the band, and if helping the band meant helping Luke . . . "All right," she said. Well, she thought, at least I'm needed.

"What's the point of sending photos?" she asked. "Aren't the tapes enough?"

He gave her a look that suggested she was naive. "This is the video age, Juliet. Ever heard of MTV? Looks sell records. Believe me, no record company wants to sign an ugly group, no matter how good the music is."

Steve dumped the stack of photos and showed her where the cassettes, labels, cover letters, wrappers, and box of cassettes were. Then he took off.

Juliet studied the photo. It was a black-and-white portrait of the band, and it had obviously been taken by a professional photographer. The shadows were in all the right places, giving the guys a pensive, somber look. The photo made a statement: Take us seriously. We're not just another rock and roll band.

Luke stood out, and not only because he was in front. Special lighting had put a slight glow on him. He appeared brooding, almost melancholy. But nonetheless sexy.

Hand-printing the labels was boring work, and

Juliet found herself almost longing to go back to her book. But this is for Luke, she scolded herself. Dani may not need you anymore, your father doesn't, either, but Luke does. So, doggedly, she plodded on. Who would have ever thought there were so many record companies in the world?

An hour later, she was immensely relieved to hear the music fade and the thunderous applause begin. She needed a break as much as the band did. A few seconds later, the guys began trooping in.

Luke wore the dazed expression she'd come to recognize. It was the way he always looked after a set, and it would take him a few minutes to come back to earth. In the meantime, she had to be content with a vague kiss.

Gary went directly to the minirefrigerator and began tossing out cans of beer. "Jules?" he asked, extending a can toward her.

"No thanks. How's the crowd?"

Before anyone could report on this, Steve came in, his face flushed with excitement. "Great set, guys. I've got someone here I want you to meet."

He presented a short, heavy-set young man with bushy eyebrows. "This is Vince Shepard. Palladium Records, A and R."

"What's A and R?" Juliet asked Luke in a whisper.

"Artists and Repertoire. He's a talent scout."

Steve was taking the man around to each band member for a personal introduction and handshake. When he reached Juliet and Luke, his voice became practically reverent. "And this . . . is Luke."

121

Vince Shepard extended his hand. "You've got a great style. Did you write all the songs?"

"With Gary," Luke said. "This is Juliet Turner."

The man glanced at her. "Do you work with the band?"

Juliet stammered. "Well, no, not exactly." Just then, Luke put his arm around her shoulders. The gesture made their relationship clear, and Vince Shepard lost interest in her. He addressed his remarks to the band members.

"I'll get right to the point. It's clear to me that you guys have a good sound. I think we can do something with you."

"Something like what?" Gary asked.

"Like cut an album. Interested?"

It didn't take long for his words to sink in. Then the guys went crazy, whooping and high-fiving and slapping each other's backs.

Vince Shepard had obviously witnessed scenes like this before. He stood there, his arms folded across his chest, beaming benignly at the guys. But his gaze lingered on Luke, as if it was Luke's reaction he was most concerned with.

Juliet looked up into Luke's face. He was the only member of the band who had remained calm, impassive. Only Juliet was aware of how his grip on her shoulder had tightened.

He leaned toward her and whispered in her ear. "What do you think?"

She was too taken aback to reply. And then she felt overwhelmed with joy. He really, really needed her.

But what did she think about the offer? What did she know about the music business? Well, Luke had to consider the future. Playing dives like Barney's wasn't much of a career.

She met his questioning eyes and nodded.

Kyle was now pouring a can of beer on Steve's head, and Michael was performing on the air guitar. Juliet kept her eyes on the record company man as he drew closer to them. "Well, Luke?" he asked softly.

Luke awarded the man a hint of a smile. "Yeah," he said. "I think we're interested."

CHAPTER · 10

It was two weeks before Juliet was able to keep her promise to Dani. But at least she was prompt, arriving at the coffee shop precisely at noon.

The Sunday brunch scene was in full force, and Juliet was afraid she wouldn't be able to get a booth. To her surprise, however, Dani had already secured one.

Juliet slid into the booth. "I can't believe it," she said to Dani. "You're here on time."

"It's the new me," Dani replied. "Reliable and dependable. What I can't believe is that you're here at all."

"Hey, come on," Juliet protested. "When I make a date, I keep it. You know that."

"I just expected you to call this morning and cancel."

"Why?"

"Because I know how things have changed for you. You're involved with Luke, the band . . ."

"But *I* haven't changed," Juliet said. "Not really. Now, I want to know everything's that going on

124

with you. We've got a lot to catch up on."

Dani tried to get the attention of a waitress, but to no avail. "Service is so slow here. What time do you have to be at Barney's?"

"I don't have to go to Barney's at all. The band's not playing there anymore. Incarnation's been signed by a record company, and they're making an album."

Dani's mouth dropped open, but before she could recover her wits and ask questions, Juliet went on. "I'll tell you all about it later. First, I want to hear about your plans." She was determined to give Dani her undivided attention.

"My plans . . . well, I've sent off applications to three schools, in Paris, the south of France, and Rome. From what the counselor at school told me, I gather that they take anybody who can pay the fees, so I figure it's going to be my choice. Basically, it boils down to whether I want to study French or Italian."

"You must be excited," Juliet commented. She smiled wistfully. "It's going to be strange for me, a year without having you around."

"My therapist says lots of kids could benefit from a year off before starting a university. Of course, I can't imagine *you* taking a year off, with your plans and goals and schedules. And a year away from you might be good for me."

Juliet's surprise was unmistakable. "What do you mean?"

"I was getting too dependent on you," Dani said, her smile taking some of the sting out of the words.

125

"I needed you too much."

"I liked being needed," Juliet said softly.

The waitress finally showed up with some menus. For the next few minutes, the girls studied their brunch options.

"What else have you been up to?" Juliet asked.

"I've been going to school, seeing the therapist, watching French and Italian movie videos, and baby-sitting for my new nephew. That's about it."

"No dates?"

"None whatsoever. But it's okay. I feel like I need this time, for myself, to figure out who I am, where I'm going. I'll bet you've got more interesting tales to tell."

The waitress returned to take their orders. Dani ordered an omelet. "I'll have the French toast," Juliet said.

"Anything to drink?"

Juliet debated mentally. Then she shook her head. "Just an orange juice, please."

"Tell me more about the band," Dani said, after the waitress left. "Is it fun, watching them record?"

"I only went the first day," Juliet told her. "Luke kept stopping the sessions and asking my advice. I was afraid I might be hurting his concentration. And I didn't want the other guys getting annoyed with me."

"But if Luke wants you there—" Dani began, but Juliet shook her head.

"I have to think of what's best for him," she said. "I hate to lie, but I made up an excuse about needing to study for exams." She sighed wearily. "I

126

hope that once they're finished with recording, things can get back to normal."

"Normal? Do you honestly think that life with a lead singer who just might become a superstar is going to become normal?"

"I guess I'll just have to play it by ear, see what happens," Juliet said.

Dani's eyes glinted mischievously. "No plans? No schedules?"

Juliet had to laugh. "How can I make any plans when I don't know what's going to happen from week to week?"

Their food appeared. As they ate, conversation turned to lighter topics—graduation, only a month away, and the big graduation dance.

"Are you going to the dance?" Dani asked.

"I don't know. I can't picture Luke at a high school graduation dance, can you? It's strange, in a way. Just a couple of months ago, I was excited thinking about graduation. Now all I can think about is Luke's album coming out. If it flops, how is he going to feel? If it's a success, will it change him? Why are you looking at me like that?"

Dani opened her mouth, then closed it.

"What? Tell me," Juliet demanded.

"Well, you sound like you're holding yourself responsible for him. Like you're in charge of his life."

"He depends on me," Juliet defended herself. "And he needs me. What's wrong with that?"

She must have spoken more sharply than she intended, because Dani changed the subject. "Do you want coffee?"

She did, but she was itching to get home. Luke usually called when Vince the slave driver gave them a break. "Let's have it back at my place. Dad would love to see you."

They paid and left. "What's happening with your dad and— what's that woman's name?"

"Eleanor. They're still going strong. They're together all the time."

"You mean he's not buried in his books anymore?"

"Oh, he still works a lot. But she's filled a big gap in his life. They make each other happy."

Her statement was confirmed when they arrived at Juliet's home and discovered Dr. Turner and Eleanor sitting together out back in the garden. They both seemed unusually happy to see her.

"You're just in time!" her father cried out. He hurried into the house.

"In time for what?" Juliet asked Eleanor.

She smiled. "We're about to have a celebration." There was an odd hint of anxiety in her voice. Dr. Turner returned bearing a tray with four glasses.

"Champagne!" Dani exclaimed. "What's the occasion? Did you finish your book?"

"It's something a bit more romantic than even the Romantic poets," Dr. Turner told her. He looked at Eleanor expectantly.

"David, why don't you tell our news?"

"Wait a minute," Dani interrupted. "Is this a family thing? Should I make myself scarce?"

"Of course not," Dr. Turner said. "You're Juliet's best friend, you're like family." But he addressed

128

his announcement more to Juliet. "Eleanor has consented to become my wife."

It wasn't an entirely unexpected announcement, but Juliet was elated nonetheless.

"I'm so happy for you both!" she cried out, while Dani was squealing "Congratulations!" And the next few moments were taken up with hugs and kisses and cries of joy.

"When is this event going to take place?" Dani asked.

"As soon as the term's over, next month, hopefully," Eleanor said. "I think we'll just have a small ceremony with family and friends. Small, but elegant."

Juliet nodded enthusiastically. Something else occurred to her. "Where will you live?"

"Here," her father said. "Eleanor's going to sell her house, it's too big."

Juliet nodded slowly. Eleanor rose and put an arm around her. "I hope that doesn't bother you. I know you've always been the woman of the house here . . ."

Juliet looked at her blankly. "Oh, it doesn't bother me at all, I'm glad you'll be living here. Dad, you need a bucket of ice for this champagne. I'll get it."

She went into the house, and Dani followed her. "Are you sure you feel okay about this? You look worried."

"I'm thinking about Luke," Juliet said as she pulled trays of ice out of the freezer. "If Eleanor's selling her house, he'll need a new place to live."

"Good grief!" Dani exclaimed. "You've just been told that your father is getting married. And all you can think about is where Luke is going to live!"

"I can't help it," Juliet said simply. "He's always on my mind."

"I just hope the feeling's mutual," Dani muttered. The phone rang and Juliet picked it up.

"Hello?"

"Juliet?"

"Luke!" She shot Dani a triumphant look. "Where are you?"

"At the studio, where else?"

"You sound tired."

"I am. Gary and I were up all night polishing some songs. I'm tired and I'm hungry and I miss you. I can't talk, they're yelling for me. But we're recording "Tattoo" this afternoon, and I want you here. I can't sing that song right if I'm not looking at you."

Warm tingles passed through her. "Are you sure it's all right if I'm there?"

"Of course it's all right, why wouldn't it be? Just get over here. Please."

She could hear the urgency in his voice. He needed her and that was all that mattered. "I'm on my way."

She handed the ice bucket to Dani. "I'll call you later, okay?" Then she stuck her head out the door. "I need to go meet Luke," she told her father and Eleanor. "Sorry I have to run out on you."

"That's all right, dear," her father said.

"We understand," Eleanor added with a wink.

130

Impulsively, she ran out and gave each of them a quick kiss before heading over to the driveway.

The studio was located in the south part of the Loop. The business area was deserted on Sundays, so she had no problem finding a close parking space. But she did encounter a problem in the building lobby.

"Where do you think you're going?" the guard barked as she headed toward the elevator.

"To the seventh floor," Juliet replied. "The recording studio."

"You on this list?" the guard asked, indicating a paper.

She wasn't. "Look, I'm expected up in the studio," Juliet insisted. "Call up there, ask for Luke." But the guard just shook his head.

Just then, the elevator door opened and Steve Lindsay stepped out. "Juliet!" A look of relief crossed his face. "I'm glad you're here."

She was glad to see that he wasn't annoyed at her appearance, but she was mildly surprised by the warmth of his greeting. "Hi, Steve. Could you tell this guard it's all right for me to go up to the studio?"

"Absolutely. Go on up, and see if you can get Luke to be reasonable."

"What are you talking about?" Juliet asked.

"You'll see," he said with a sigh. "I'll be back in a few minutes."

Puzzled, she went into the elevator. When the doors opened on the seventh floor, she could hear Josh's voice.

"Look, man, what's your problem? Can't you see that this could be good for us?"

Stepping out of the elevator, she identified the next voice as Vince's. "It's going to give us an edge, buddy. It'll be noticed, it'll give people something to talk about."

Then she heard Luke. "Forget it. I'm not doing that damned song."

No one saw her at first when she appeared at the doorway to the control room. Josh was arguing heatedly. "We need it, Luke! No one's heard of us outside of Chicago. Don't you want to see this album go gold?"

"Forget gold!" Vince chimed in. "We're talking platinum here!"

"You thought we were good enough to sign without doing this kind of crap," Luke shot back.

"Quality doesn't always translate to sales," Vince declared. "There are plenty of good new bands. You need something to make you stand out."

"And we need one more track, anyway," Gary offered.

Luke's eyes were streaked with red, but he didn't act exhausted. If anything, he seemed a little wired. "We've got a dozen tunes to choose from. And I want "Tattoo" on this album."

"That's a love song," Kyle said. "We need a power tune."

"It's not going to kill you to do one lousy cover," Michael added. "It's not going to damage your precious integrity."

Vince spotted Juliet. "Judy, would you talk some

132

sense into this guy?"

"My name is Juliet." She strode forward and took her place by Luke's side. "What's going on?" She was totally bewildered. Had the guys been arguing like this all week?

"They want to do a Luke Dennison number," Luke told her.

"Why?"

"It's a good angle," Vince began, but Luke cut him short.

"It's a gimmick. I don't do gimmicks." He turned to Gary. "We don't need this. We're good, we've got good music. I don't want to beg for comparisons."

Gary seemed torn, but he appeared to side with the others. "Can you talk some sense into him?" he pleaded with Juliet.

"I think he's making perfectly good sense," Juliet replied. "He's not Luke Dennison, and I don't understand why you want him to imitate a dead rock star."

Vince forced a smile. "Sweetie, do you have any idea how much interest there is now in Luke Dennison? He's a cult figure! We can use that to our advantage!"

Josh clenched his fists. "Luke, we agreed that Incarnation is going to make all decisions together. The other guys want to do the Luke Dennison song."

"Fine," Luke said. "Do the cover. But you'll do it without me." He took Juliet's hand, and they walked out.

They were halfway down the hall when they heard Vince yelling. "Luke! Wait!" The plump man was out of breath by the time he reached them. He glanced furtively back at the room he'd come from, and he spoke in an undertone.

"Look, as far as I'm concerned, you *are* Incarnation. You're the one Palladium's interested in. These other guys are just along for the ride. They're replaceable."

Luke's eyes narrowed, and Vince hastily qualified that. "What I'm saying is that we want you to be happy. You don't want to do Luke Dennison? Fine, we don't do Luke Dennison. Now, why don't you take a break. Have a drink, cool off."

Luke nodded shortly, and led Juliet into another room. It was a lounge, with a full bar set up. Luke went directly to that and poured himself a shot of something. He gulped it down.

"Sorry," he said to Juliet. "You want a drink?"

"No, thanks." She edged closer. "Luke, have you guys been fighting a lot?"

"Some." He ran his fingers through his hair. "Why haven't you been here all week?"

"I told you. I was studying for exams." She hated lying to him. "And . . . I didn't want to get in the way."

"Get in the way?" His eyebrows shot up. "Juliet, you're a part of me. How could you ever be in my way?"

"I'm here now," she said warmly. "Have you eaten? You want me to get you something?"

"No, I'm not hungry." He poured another drink. "I want to show you something." He began unbuttoning his shirt.

"Luke!" Did he really expect them to make love next door to the studio? "Not here!"

He was smiling as he pulled his shirt open. Juliet put a hand to her mouth. There, on the left side of his chest, in deep blood red letters was a word: Juliet.

"I slipped out a few days ago and had it done."

Juliet reached out and touched it tentatively. "It's real, isn't it. Not one of those decals . . ."

"It's real." He took her fingers from his chest and kissed them, one at a time. With each kiss, a delicious tickle went up her arm.

"Luke!" Steve burst in. "Ready to make some music, pal?"

Luke relinquished Juliet's hand. "Yeah." He buttoned his shirt without taking his eyes off Juliet. "Steve will show you where to stand. I want to be able to see you."

"Okay."

"Juliet . . ."

"Hmm?"

He spoke quietly. "I wish they wouldn't push this Luke Dennison thing. Maybe I don't know who I am, but I'm not Luke Dennison."

"Of course you're not," Juliet said soothingly.

But his eyes were still on her, and there was still the question in them.

"Luke Dennison is dead," Juliet said. "You're alive."

Finally, he nodded. They went back down to the studio. While Luke joined the other band members, Steve and Juliet went into the control room where they could see the band through a glass panel.

135

"Steve . . ."

"What?"

"When they finish recording—what happens next?"

"We make a couple of videos, try to line up some TV appearances. Probably go on a concert tour."

A tour. Juliet swallowed. "For—for how long?"

"Depends how well the album does. Six months, maybe longer." He moved away from her to talk with Vince.

Six months, maybe longer. Without Luke. Juliet wished there was an extra chair for her to sit in. Her legs felt wobbly. Don't cross bridges before you come to them, she told herself. Through the glass pane, Luke smiled at her. She smiled back.

"Let's try a run-through," Vince said into a microphone.

Luke began to sing. *You pierce my skin, and etch your name on my heart. And I'll live with the pain, just to have you there, where no one can touch you, and you can never go away. You're in me, my tattoo. I'll never lose you.*

No, you'll never lose me, she thought. Not for six months, maybe longer. Not ever.

CHAPTER · 11

Dear Dani,

Or maybe I should write, *Bonjour, mon amie!* I suppose you're speaking nothing but French by now. After all, you've been there two months already.

I can't believe I haven't seen you since the day we graduated. I'm sorry it's taken me so long to write, but my life has been crazy. I don't know where to begin.

I could start off by telling you that as I write this, I'm sitting on an airplane on my way to New York City. But maybe I'd better go back a couple of months, so you'll understand why.

Incarnation's first album was released at the end of June, right after you left. They made a video too, just a quickie—it showed the guys in the studio, lip-synching to one of the songs, "Edge of the Sky," and pretending to play their instruments. Personally, I thought it was pretty feeble. But it caught on.

Suddenly, every time I turned on MTV, there was Luke and the band. The album was in record-store windows, and it was reviewed in *Spin*. I didn't realize how popular the band had become until one day when Luke and I were walking on Michigan Avenue and kids kept stopping him and asking for his autograph.

It's strange, though. With the video playing regularly on national television, you'd think someone would have recognized Luke by now. But no one has, and Luke has never remembered anything about his life before that night on Lake Shore Drive.

Do I care? I'm not sure. Of course, I'm curious. But we're so happy with each other that I sometimes think I'd just as soon not know anything about his life before we were together. I don't know if the amnesia bothers him—he doesn't talk about it. Sometimes, though, he gets this distant look in his eyes, like he's not really there, and I wonder if that's what he's thinking about.

Anyway, Dad and Eleanor got married, and it was a lovely wedding. I'm sorry you missed it. Eleanor sold her house, so Luke had to move in with a couple of guys in the band who had an apartment. But guess where he stayed while Eleanor and Dad were on their two-week honeymoon!

The record company decided to send the group on tour. Luke said he couldn't stand the thought of us being separated for that long. I couldn't bear the thought of it, either. Even Vince, the guy from Palladium, and Steve, the manager, wanted me to come— they were afraid Luke would be miserable without me and it would affect his performances.

So I decided to put off college for a semester and tour with the band. I expected my father to be really upset by this, but he was unbelievably understanding. He said travel was a learning experience in itself, that I was mature and responsible enough to handle it. I think Dad actually approves of the idea that I'm finally, for the first time in my life, doing something sort of unpredictable!

I'm thinking of asking Vince or Steve if there's some sort of job I can do during the tour—maybe keeping track of ticket sales, or something like that. I can't just tag along behind Luke and the guys, like some kind of groupie.

Anyway, here I am, on my way to the first gig. I'll write again, and let you know how it goes. Love, Juliet.

Juliet folded the pages, stuck them in an envelope, and put the envelope in her purse. She peered out the tiny window at the fluffy white clouds below. She began playing an old childhood game, trying to decide what each cloud looked like—a rabbit? A horse? But all she could come up with were formless wisps of cotton.

"Would you like something to drink?"

She turned to the flight attendant. "No, thank you."

The woman's eyes lingered on Luke, asleep in his aisle seat. "Well, let me know if there's anything I can get either of you."

Flight attendants were certainly more attentive in first class, Juliet thought. Or maybe it was just having Luke by her side that called forth an attendant every few minutes.

She looked out the window again. The plane seemed to be inside the clouds now. Everything was a blur. So here she was, on her way to New York City. She'd never been there before. Neither had Luke—as far as either of them knew.

She rose and carefully climbed over him to go to the bathroom. Across the aisle and several rows in front of them, Josh and Michael were tossing back drinks and flirting with a couple of very young teenage girls. On her way to the bathroom, she passed Vince and Steve. Steve was sleeping, but Vince caught her arm as she moved by.

"How's Luke doing?"

"He's fine. He's sleeping."

"Good, good," Vince said. "He needs all the rest

he can get. The schedule's pretty tight in New York. Interviews, photo sessions, and all that."

Juliet glanced at the other band members. "Maybe you should tell them to get some rest, too."

"I'm not worried about them," Vince said. "Just between us, sweetie, Luke's the star of this group. He might not know that yet, but he will, very soon."

"Vince, I wanted to ask you if there's something I can do during the tour."

He looked at her blankly. "Do?"

"I need to keep busy. I thought maybe you could give me some sort of assignment, a job that I could do for Palladium."

Vince was smiling. "You already have a job, Juliet."

Now it was her turn to look blank. "What's that?"

"Taking care of Luke."

Vince made it sound as though Luke were a kitten who had to be fed on a regular basis. For a moment, she thought he was joking. But Vince looked completely serious. She smiled uncertainly. "I'll see you later."

She moved on, passing the two teenage girls, who were now slobbering over Gary, and went into the tiny bathroom. As she brushed her hair, she thought about what Vince had said, and she frowned. He'd basically told her that she was a baby-sitter—as if Luke needed one!

Quickly, to ease her discomfort, she began to rationalize his words. Palladium had invested a lot of money into a new group. They just wanted to make sure it paid off. They wanted Luke to be

141

happy—if he was happy, he'd perform well, write new songs, and make the group a big hit. And Vince knew that Luke was happy when she was with him. That's all it was.

Still, baby-sitting wasn't exactly the kind of job she'd had in mind.

When she came back down the aisle, she discovered those same two teenage girls, now bent over Luke. "It *is* him," one of them giggled.

Juliet tapped her on the shoulder. "Excuse me."

The girl turned. "That's Luke, isn't it? We want his autograph."

"He's sleeping," Juliet said impatiently. "Can't you see that?"

The girls looked at her with interest. "You his girlfriend?" the other one asked.

Where was the flight attendant when she needed her, Juliet fumed. "Please go away. You're going to wake him."

"We already did," the first girl announced in triumph.

Luke's eyes were only half open, but he managed a smile and accepted the pen the girl thrust at him. After securing his signature, they scurried away, still giggling.

Juliet got into her seat, and Luke took her hand.

"I'm sorry about that," Juliet said. "I was in the bathroom, or I would have kept them away."

"It's okay," Luke replied. "You're not my baby-sitter. I guess I have to get used to it."

She wished Vince had heard that! Impulsively, she leaned over and kissed Luke. "Thank you."

"For what?"

She grinned. "For being you."

He rolled his eyes. "Whoever that is."

The flight attendant returned. "We're beginning our descent. Please put your trays up and return your seats to the upright position." As Juliet obeyed, she noticed with some amusement that the flight attendant was taking care of Luke's tray and seat herself.

I'm going to have to get used to *that*, she thought. The women. At least Luke wasn't taking the attention seriously.

The plane landed, and everything proceeded smoothly. As Vince promised, there was someone from Palladium Records waiting for them at the gate. He ushered them out of the airport to two waiting limousines, and their luggage was brought out.

Juliet marveled. Not only was she in New York, she was arriving in Manhattan in a limousine. Luke seemed less impressed by the fancy car. He settled back, looking like he'd been riding in limousines for years.

Steve got in with them and sat in the seat facing them. As soon as the limo took off, he started talking. "Okay, it's one o'clock now, and we'll be at the hotel by two. The reporter from *Disc* is showing up at three, and the photographer at five. The band needs to be at Radio City Music Hall at seven for a sound check."

"Reporters and photographers?" Luke made a face. "I don't want to have to do that crap. Let Vince handle it."

143

"We got to have the publicity, man," Steve said. "Right, Juliet?"

Juliet looked at him in bewilderment. "I don't know anything about publicity, Steve."

Steve gave her a meaningful look, and nodded toward Luke, who still wore a disgruntled expression. She realized Steve wanted her to encourage Luke to cooperate.

"I guess it's important," she said slowly.

She looked out at the passing scene while Steve continued to go over the schedule with Luke. They were in Manhattan now, and it looked just like it did in the movies—big buildings, lots of traffic, hordes of people on the street, all moving fast.

The limousine pulled up in front of a non-descript building. The door was opened by the chauffeur, and they were whisked inside. Juliet got a fleeting glimpse of glass and chrome in a lobby that seemed rather grand, but there was no chance to have a good look around. Vince had already secured their keys, and he escorted them to the top floor. A bellhop followed with their luggage.

"This is your suite," the bellhop said as he opened the door. Since Vince had Luke deep in conversation, the bellhop showed the room to Juliet.

There was the main room, furnished like a living room, and two bedrooms, each with its own bath. While the bellhop pointed out the features of the suite, Juliet tried to listen in on what Vince was telling Luke.

"This reporter, he's going to want background on

144

you. I'm thinking that maybe you shouldn't mention the amnesia."

Luke was gazing around the room, his forehead puckered. Juliet wondered if he'd heard Vince.

"Why shouldn't he mention the amnesia?" she asked Vince.

"I don't know, it sounds hokey, like something out of a soap opera."

"But the reporter will ask about his background, won't he?" Juliet persisted. "Luke, what do you think?"

Luke turned slowly. "About what?"

"Vince thinks you shouldn't tell the reporter you have amnesia."

Luke's eyes narrowed. "But that's what I have, Vince. You think I'm faking amnesia?"

"No, no," Vince said hastily. "But when the reporter asks about your background, you could just be evasive. It'll give you an image of mystery. Not a bad image for a rock star."

Luke had moved away from him and was now staring out the window. "I *am* a mystery," he said.

"Well, just be careful about what you say, okay? I'll be back in an hour with the other guys and the reporter."

The bellhop was standing by the door. "Is there anything I can bring you?"

"This room . . ." Luke murmured.

The man's face fell. "You're not happy with it, sir?"

Luke was rubbing his forehead. Juliet gazed at him worriedly for a moment, and then turned to the man. "I don't think we need anything else," she began, but Luke broke in. "Yeah. A bottle of tequila." He gave the man some money and the man took off.

"Since when did you start drinking tequila?" Juliet asked.

"I don't know. It just popped into my head. Come here."

He buried his head in her hair and whispered in her hair. "It's happening . . . so fast. I couldn't get through this without you."

A moment later she was pushing him away. "Let's not start something we don't have time to finish. You have to shower and get ready for your interview. And I'm going to take off."

"Why? Where are you going?" He clutched her arm tightly. What was that in his voice—fear? It almost sounded like panic. His grip on her arm was tightening.

"Luke, you're hurting me!"

He let go immediately. "I'm sorry. What are you going to do, sightsee?" Now his voice was normal.

"Yes, just walk around."

"Be careful, okay? I'll see you later." He strode off toward the bedroom.

As she went down the elevator and out of the hotel, she pondered Luke's peculiar reactions. He was nervous, she concluded. This was a new and strange experience for him. She couldn't expect him to stay calm and cool with all these new pressures.

But she'd help him deal with it. He'd get used to

it all, eventually, and everything would be fine. Having made that optimistic decision, she set off to enjoy her free afternoon.

It was easy to kill an afternoon in New York. Armed with a map and a tourist guide, Juliet headed first to the Metropolitan Museum of Art, where she spent a couple of happy hours just roaming from room to room. Then she strolled down Fifth Avenue, window-shopping along the way. She stopped to see St. Patrick's Cathedral and the Empire State Building. Then, on a whim, she decided to take a look at the place where the band would be playing that night.

Thirty minutes later, she stood across the street from Radio City Music Hall and stared at the marquee proclaiming "Tonight and Tomorrow— Incarnation." She hoped it wasn't as huge inside as it looked from the outside. How awful it would be for the band, playing to a half-empty auditorium after packing in the crowds back home.

She crossed the street and peered through the glass pane of a door. A teenage boy standing under the awning spoke.

"A hundred bucks."

Startled, Juliet clutched her handbag to her chest.

The boy emerged from the shadows. "Tickets for Incarnation. Tonight. A hundred bucks each."

Juliet was shocked. "This place is charging a hundred dollars for a rock concert?"

"It's sold out. But I've got tickets to sell." He pulled two from his pocket.

Juliet examined them. The price was clearly indicated— twenty-five dollars. She gave the boy a reproving look. "Nobody's going to give you a hundred dollars for a twenty-five dollar ticket."

"Wanna bet?"

His assumption was confirmed in the next few seconds, as two boys came toward him. "You the scalper?" one of them asked.

"Yeah. A hundred bucks."

Juliet watched in amazement as money changed hands. "See?" the ticket seller said to her.

"I see." She was reeling as she walked away. That huge theater, sold out. Kids paying a hundred dollars for a ticket.

But even knowing this didn't prepare her for the reality that evening. Looking back from her third-row center seat, the sea of expectant faces stretched out endlessly. The air was punctuated by whistles and occasional shrieks.

None of these noises were coming from the seats around her. As Vince explained to her, the best seats were held for record-company executives, critics, and celebrities.

"It doesn't seem fair," she commented, waving toward the audience behind her. "Those are the real fans."

"But these are the people who count. Recognize that guy?" He was indicating a grizzled older man who was taking a seat in front of him. With his long gray hair pulled back in a ponytail and the beads around his neck, he looked like an aging hippie.

"No."

"Ever heard of High Times?"

"Of course."

"That's Mac Stewart."

"You're kidding," Juliet exclaimed. "I didn't even know he was still alive." High Times had been one of the most famous bands of the late 1960s. Juliet recalled a music documentary she'd once seen that described High Times as the epitome of the "drugs-sex-rock and roll" mentality. Mac Stewart had been the lead guitarist.

"What's he doing here?" Juliet wondered aloud.

"We wanted him to hear the band. He's still got a following, so we thought maybe Luke should call him up to the stage tomorrow night."

"Why?"

"He was a good buddy of Luke Dennison."

Juliet spoke sharply. "What does that have to do with Incarnation?"

Just then the lights went down, and the noise level went up. One by one, each band member was hit with a spotlight. Luke was lit up last, and the screams hit a level that made Juliet jump. The concert began.

But concert wasn't the right word for what happened on the stage over the next two hours. It was something between an embrace and an assault on the senses. Juliet didn't know if it was the space, or the sound system, or the huge audience, but Incarnation became larger than life.

And Luke—Luke was dazzling, a mesmerizing presence that entranced the crowd. His voice was electric, like pure, raw energy. So many times Juliet had heard him and he'd made her quiver. Now, her entire body trembled in amazement.

He was all over the stage, moving, twirling, leaping. He crooned and raged and tore into his songs as if they'd never been sung before. Each tune was imbued with a new abandon, a new and higher level of passion.

And when he sang *her* song, "Tattoo", it was a caress, a physical thing that sent shock waves through the audience—and through Juliet. When it was over—after two encores and pleas for more—she was drained, exhausted, as if she herself had been up on that stage with him. The audience was still shrieking, "Luke, Luke, Luke," as Vince took her arm and led her away.

It seemed like half the audience was backstage. Juliet edged through the crowd of fans, searching. "Kyle! Kyle, where's Luke?"

Kyle, waving a bottle of something, couldn't hear her. Frantically, Juliet pushed and shoved against people who were pushing and shoving her. She spotted Gary. "Where's Luke?"

"Dressing room," Gary yelled back.

She managed to get alongside the wall, and tried to orient herself. Finally, she discovered the entrance to the dressing room. It was hard opening the door with the crush of people pressed against it, but somehow, she eventually found herself inside.

Luke was slumped in a chair, his eyes glazed and unfocused. He didn't seem aware of Juliet's presence. The old rocker, Mac, was there, too, sitting next to him, speaking in a low, growly voice.

"It was like seeing him up there. He's living in you, man."

"Luke," Juliet said. His eyes moved slowly in her direction. Then he stretched out an arm toward her. She went to him, bent down, and kissed his forehead.

"This your old lady?" Mac Stewart asked.

The phrase made her shudder, but she knew they'd used expressions like that in his day. "I'm Juliet Turner. It's a pleasure to meet you." As she spoke, she kept her focus on Luke. With relief, she saw his eyes clearing, his smile becoming natural. "This is the woman I love, Mac," he said.

Mac nodded and wagged a finger playfully at Juliet. "You better take care of this guy."

Juliet smiled uncertainly.

"She didn't, you know," he continued.

"Who?" Juliet asked.

"Gloria. She let him go right down the drain. She followed him there, too."

Juliet wondered if he was stoned. He went on talking.

"He needed care. He was brilliant, there was a fire inside him. Don't put it out, just don't let it devour him. Please?"

Her eyes darted back and forth between Mac and Luke. Luke was listening intently. Did this make more sense to him than it did to her, or was he just being polite?

"Please," he said again, to Juliet. "I don't want to lose him again."

The door to the dressing room jerked open. "Hey, get moving," Gary yelled. "They're giving us a big party."

"A big party," Mac Stewart mused. "Like old times, huh, Luke?"

Juliet took Luke's hand. "Luke, come on, let's go."

He rose obediently. They left Mac staring at the empty seat as if Luke were still sitting there. At the door, Luke turned and looked back at him. Juliet tightened her grip on his hand and gazed up.

Luke shook his head and smiled. "Crazy old man," he said.

CHAPTER · 12

Luke was still sleeping the next morning, long after Juliet had showered and dressed and eaten the breakfast delivered by room service. She couldn't blame him for sleeping late. At the party Palladium Records had thrown for Incarnation, he'd been the center of attention.

When the phone rang, she rushed to get it before it woke him.

"Hello?"

"Hi, Juliet, let me talk to Luke."

"He's not up yet, Steve."

There was a sigh of exasperation on the other end. "Juliet, it's almost noon. Haven't you looked at the schedule? Get him up and tell him the photographer's going to be there in half an hour."

So this is my job, Juliet thought unhappily. She managed to keep any irritation out of her tone. "I thought the photos were taken yesterday."

"The magazine wants more, of Luke alone. Just get him ready, okay? Thanks." He broke the connection.

Juliet replaced the receiver and grimaced. She hated to wake him.

But she didn't have to. The bedroom door opened.

"Good morning," she called out brightly. "That was Steve on the phone. Some photographer's coming here in half an hour to take more pictures of you." She paused. "Just you. Not the whole band."

He didn't seem surprised. He kissed her, and said, "I'm sorry about last night."

She knew what he meant. They'd been separated the whole evening.

"You've got nothing to be sorry for," she assured him. "People wanted to meet you." She struck a pose. "You're a star, Luke!"

He laughed. "I'll make it up to you tonight. After the concert. There's another party, but we don't have to go. It will be just us."

"I'd like that." She tried to reconcile the sweet, apologetic person standing before her with the wild rocker on stage last night. It was impossible. "You'd better get ready for the photographer."

"Right," Luke replied, and then struck an exaggerated glamour pose. "After all, I'm a star." He disappeared back into the bedroom, and Juliet turned on the television. Hitting the remote control buttons, she searched for a news program. She caught the end of one.

"And now, for news from the entertainment world, here's Mark Dobson. What's happening, Mark?"

"Well, Bob, if you weren't at Radio City Music Hall last night, you missed some real excitement. Incarnation is one of the hottest new bands to hit the scene in a long time. They're getting noticed not only because of their music, but because their lead singer, Luke, bears an almost eerie resemblance—"

There was a knock. Juliet switched off the TV and went to the door. A woman stood there, with a camera around her neck and her arms filled with lighting equipment. "Hi, I'm Karen Hudson." She flashed a card that identified her as a member of the press.

"Come in. Luke's getting dressed."

The woman swept by her and began setting up equipment. At one point, she gave Juliet a swift, appraising glance.

She thinks I'm a groupie, Juliet thought. She introduced herself. "I came with Luke from Chicago."

"Keeping an eye on him, huh?" She laughed. "Listen, I've been there. Of course, it was a lot wilder back in the early seventies."

Now that Karen Hudson was standing in a bright light, Juliet could see that she was fortyish. "Have you known a lot of rock stars?"

"I've been shooting them since the late sixties. And I'll tell you something. Your friend Luke is going to be big."

Juliet smiled. "He does have a good voice."

"It's more than that," the woman said dryly.

Luke emerged from the bedroom and the

woman greeted him crisply. "Stand over here, in the light." She took a few quick shots, and then cocked her head to one side. "Unbutton your shirt."

Luke obliged. She clicked away for a while, then paused again. "Take it off."

Juliet supposed rock stars did have to be sex symbols. Luke slipped his shirt off, and Karen raised the camera. Then she put it down.

"So you've got one, too."

"One what?" Luke asked.

She nodded toward the tattoo on his chest. Luke grinned.

"You mean there's another rock star running around with his girlfriend's name over his heart?"

"There was. You know who I'm talking about."

"No," Luke said. "I don't." But his smile was fading.

The photographer uttered a short laugh. "Give me a break. Luke Dennison had Gloria's name in the exact same spot on his chest."

"I didn't know that," Luke said.

She studied him skeptically, then shrugged. "Maybe you didn't. Not that many people knew about it. He wouldn't let anyone shoot him with his shirt off."

"How did you know about the tattoo, then?" Juliet asked.

Karen winked. "I was a pretty wild woman myself back then. And Luke Dennison wasn't exactly faithful to his Gloria."

"Why wouldn't he let you take his picture with his shirt off?" Luke asked.

Karen shrugged. "Either he was embarrassed about his skinny body, or he didn't want to get his groupies too worked up."

Luke slipped his shirt back on and began buttoning it.

"Hey, I'm not done," Karen objected.

"Maybe I shouldn't be doing this either," Luke said.

"Why not?" Karen asked.

"Well, my body's pretty skinny, too . . ."

Juliet noticed that he was rubbing his forehead again. "Luke, do you want an aspirin?"

"No."

Karen was gazing at him with a slight smile. But all she said was, "I think you need some makeup. You're too pale."

Juliet wished *she* had something to do. "Would you like a drink?" she asked the photographer.

"Diet soda, if you've got it."

Juliet went behind the well-stocked bar. "Luke?"

"A shot of tequila."

He hadn't even had any breakfast yet, but she didn't want to say anything in front of Karen.

"Tequila, huh?" The photographer smirked. "Is that part of the game plan?"

"What game plan?" Luke asked.

"That's what Dennison drank. Tequila. Come on, you must have known that. Sales of tequila hit an all-time high in 1970."

She was beginning to annoy Juliet. "Luke wasn't around in 1970."

Karen's expression was cynical. "I'm assuming

Palladium Records filled you in on the details. This is your gimmick, right? Doing a Luke Dennison thing? Don't worry, your secret is safe with me."

"That's ridiculous," Juliet snapped. She looked at Luke to see how he was taking this. He didn't seem angry, but he was gazing at Karen intently.

"What was he like?" he asked her.

"Dennison?" She sipped her soda. "He was . . . fire and ice. Devil and angel. Totally unpredictable. Onstage, he could drive an audience into a frenzy. People stormed the stage, just wanting to get close to him, to touch him. There's never been anyone like him before. Or since." She took another sip. "Until now."

"No one stormed the stage last night," Luke said.

"Excuse me," Juliet said suddenly. "I think I'll go out for a little while." The direction of the conversation was making her uncomfortable.

"Where are you going?" Luke asked in alarm.

"Just to the bookstore across the street," Juliet said. "I need something to read." Then, remembering what Karen's words about her relationship with Luke Dennison had implied, she added, "I'll be back in fifteen minutes, I promise." She kissed him lightly on the cheek.

The photographer was looking at her in amusement. "If you're going to pull off a Gloria impersonation, you'll have to be a lot more passionate than that."

Juliet gave her a withering look and walked out. What nonsense, she thought as she went across the street to the bookstore. People were so cynical in this business.

In the bookstore, she browsed for a while, and picked up a couple of mysteries. Then she wandered over to the biography section and scanned the titles. Maybe she'd been looking for it, maybe not—in any case, the book stood out, and she took it off the shelf.

Out of Control; A New and Revealing Look into the Life and Death of Luke Dennison. The same one Dani had picked up that day last winter in Chicago.

She paid for her purchases and went back to the hotel. Only Luke was in the room. "She's gone," Juliet said in relief.

"You didn't like her?"

"I didn't like what she was saying. Honestly, Luke, she practically accused you of trying to impersonate Luke Dennison. It's not as if you had plastic surgery or something."

Luke went to the window and stared out. "It's strange, though. Isn't it? The tattoo. Tequila."

"Coincidences," Juliet said.

"And this room . . . "

"What about this room?" she asked.

"When I first walked in, I felt like I'd been here before. And get this. Karen said this is the very room Luke Dennison stayed in almost twenty-five years ago. Pretty spooky, huh?"

"Another coincidence," Juliet declared. "First of all, how do you know she was telling the truth? She seems determined to compare you to Dennison, so she'd probably say anything. As for the room looking familiar, all hotel rooms look pretty much alike, and you probably stayed in a similar one before. Okay?"

She watched as he eased himself into a chair, rested an elbow on the chair arm, and began rubbing his brow. "You keep doing that," she said in concern. "Are you having bad headaches?"

"It's like . . . I'm trying to remember something."

She went behind him, and put her hands on both sides of his head. Gently, she rubbed his temples. He reached up and clutched one of her hands.

"What am I doing? I don't want people to think I'm imitating him."

"When I first met you," Juliet began slowly, "that's what I thought. But Keith said . . ." She stopped, thinking it would bother Luke to hear about her old boyfriend. But he inclined his head toward hers.

"What did Keith say?"

"Maybe, before you lost your memory, you were a fan of Luke Dennison. You might have known a lot about him. All that information, it could be buried in your subconscious, and you do what he did without even realizing it. Like drink tequila."

"I guess that's possible," he said. He didn't sound convinced.

"Don't worry about it," Juliet ordered him. "People will talk about the resemblance for a while. Then the novelty will wear off, and they'll come around to accepting you for who you are."

"Whoever that is," he murmured. He noticed the

bag she'd dropped on the floor. "What did you buy?"

"Just some books. Mysteries." She left him and took the bag into her bedroom, before he could ask to see them. Removing the Luke Dennison book, she shook her head ruefully. Why had she bought this trash? How would Luke feel if he saw she had it? She considered dropping it in the wastebasket, but he might see it there.

She went to the closet, opened her suitcase, and tossed it in. Then she slammed the suitcase shut.

* * *

That evening, Juliet decided not to sit in the audience at the performance. She took one of the mysteries she'd bought, and planted herself in the dressing room. It wasn't easy to ignore the sounds that filtered backstage, even with the door closed. With effort, she managed to shut out the music and applause and shrieking.

But suddenly, about an hour into the concert, she realized that the sounds had changed. She wasn't hearing music—just screams—louder, frantic screams—and pounding, like thousands of feet running.

Frightened, she leaped up. Visions of a disaster —fire, a roof cave-in—flew through her mind as she ran out of the room. She collided with Steve, pale and shaken.

"They're storming the stage!"

She ran down the hall. As she approached the

161

entrance to the stage, the noise level became unbearable. Uniformed guards were escorting stunned band members off the stage. Luke appeared, with a guard on each arm. His shirt hung in tattered rags.

"Luke! Are you all right?" Juliet cried out in panic. "What happened?"

He didn't speak. The guards pulled him down the hall toward the dressing room. She was only able to get one quick look at his face. At least there were no cuts or bruises. And he didn't look pale or stunned. Not even surprised.

She hurried past the guards into the dressing room. To her surprise, Luke still didn't seem shaken. If anything, he seemed wired as he changed his clothes. "Ready to party?" he asked.

"Luke, you said we could be alone tonight," she protested. "And you need some rest."

"Just for a little while," he said.

She looked at him quizzically. "Since when did you turn into such a party animal?"

"I don't know," he said carelessly. "I'm just in the mood tonight."

She toyed with a bottle of hair gel on the dressing room table. "But I'm not. Maybe I'll just go back to the hotel." She made the mistake of looking into his eyes.

"No, Juliet, please. Come with me."

She sighed. "But we won't stay long, okay?"

"Okay."

Three hours later, she was slumped in a chair, trying to keep her eyes open. The party was going strong, and so was Luke. At least, she assumed he was going strong. She hadn't seen him in over an hour.

She didn't know who was throwing this party. It was different than the one the night before. That one had been noisy and lively, but this one was manic.

The nightclub, or bar, or whatever the place was, had been designed to look like a seventies disco, complete with strobe lights. Bizarre people floated around her, blending together as if in some psychedelic kaleidoscope. A woman with a snake tattoo crawling up her arm, a man with green, spiked hair, a woman in black leather and chains carrying a whip. Someone she couldn't identify as male or female was dancing on a table with fire batons.

A man and a woman planted themselves at her table. The woman poured a small amount of white powder onto the table, and began using a matchbook to separate the stuff into lines. The man rolled up a twenty-dollar bill into a straw.

Juliet got up.

"Have some, honey?" the woman asked.

"No, thanks. I need to find Luke."

The man laughed. "Good luck."

The flashing lights, the throbbing music, and the gyrating bodies on the dance floor disoriented her. But she did find him, eventually. And he seemed awfully happy to see her.

He stretched out his arms to her. "You're glowing tonight."

"It's the lighting," Juliet said.

"No, you're radiant, you're shooting sparks." He stroked her head. "I love how your hair feels."

"Thank you," she said stupidly. His smile was unwavering, pasted on his face. His eyes were cloudy.

Some guy Juliet had never seen before joined them. "Feeling good, Luke?"

"Ecstatic," Luke replied.

The man threw back his head and roared. "You're right on the mark, baby."

"Oh, Luke," Juliet moaned. "Let's go back to the hotel."

"I want to dance," he said. He took her in his arms, but he didn't move his feet. He simply swayed her back and forth. "Do you know how much I love you?"

"You're high," she said flatly.

"It's not a high," he whispered in her ear. "It's a happiness. That's why they call it Ecstasy."

She knew nothing she said would make sense to him in this condition, but she couldn't let him think this was okay with her. "You don't need drugs to be happy, Luke. You've got it all. Success, fame, money. Me."

"I'll be even happier when I know who I am."

"Ecstasy can't do that for you," Juliet said.

Still swaying, he didn't answer. He probably hadn't even heard her. But then, as if from a distance, his words came faintly. "It might help me deal with it. Accept it."

"Accept *what*?"

But by now, he was far away.

CHAPTER · 13

It would be easy to lose track of where you were on a concert tour, Juliet thought. After a couple of weeks, everything began to look alike—the airports, the hotel rooms, the performance spaces. Even the restaurant they were now sitting in looked like every other restaurant. So she wasn't alarmed when Luke asked, "Where are we?"

"Atlanta," she replied.

He nodded and took a long drag on his cigarette. That was another habit he'd picked up on tour, along with the tequila and Ecstasy. She hated the smell of it, and kissing him was less pleasant now. But she never said a word about any of his new inclinations anymore. The first time she had, he'd stared at her in silence. The second time, he'd cried.

"You look so tired," she said.

"I am," he admitted.

She made her next suggestion carefully. "Maybe . . . you might not want to go out after the concert tonight."

He nodded. "I'm not up for any partying."

In her eyes, he wasn't up for anything. For several days now, he seemed to be getting quieter, and his headaches, or whatever they were, had become more frequent. He was pale, his eyes were haggard. He could he possibly perform tonight? His plate was barely touched. He hadn't had enough energy to eat.

"Let's go back to the room," she said. "You could take a little nap."

He nodded again. Juliet signed their room number to the check, and they left. Unfortunately, they had to go through the lobby to get to the elevator, with the usual consequences.

"There he is!" the now-familiar cry came. Instantly, Luke was surrounded by a bevy of teenage girls.

"Please, leave him alone," Juliet begged, but she knew even as she spoke that her plea was futile. Luke began signing album covers, notebooks, whatever they thrust at him. Most of the girls were giggling like hyenas. But one thin, fragile girl, who couldn't have been more than fifteen, had tears running down her face.

"It *is* him," she sobbed. "You're real. You're not a ghost."

Juliet was reminded of Dani, that night months ago at Barney's. "Luke, let's go," she said urgently.

"I want to take a picture," a girl cried out, raising her camera. To her friends, she said, "If he's a vampire, he won't show up in the photo."

"Luke, come on!" Juliet put a hand on his arm

166

and tugged. She didn't let go until they were safely on the elevator. "I can't believe this nonsense. Ghosts, vampires . . ."

Luke was less disturbed. "They just want something to believe in."

They emerged from the elevator to find Vince banging on their door. "Check this out," he called, waving a magazine at them. He had more under his arm.

They went into the room, and Vince tossed the magazines on the desk. "It's the interview, the one you did in New York."

Luke took one and sat down. At the desk with Vince, Juliet scanned the article. The interview part was pretty ordinary. Gary had done most of the talking, about how the band got together, their musical goals, and all that. The writer's review of that first concert was complimentary. But the conclusion wasn't very kind.

> Luke's songs are original compositions, but his remarkable resemblance, both in terms of his physical makeup and his onstage presence, to the late Luke Dennison poses the inevitable question— what's going on here? At the opening-night show, rumors were flying, and a variety of suggestions were proposed by the fans. He's Dennison's ghost. He's a reincarnation, thus the name of the band. He's a mental case who *thinks* he's Luke Dennison. And then there's the more

plausible explanation, that it's all hype,
that this is some outrageous contrivance
dreamed up by an unscrupu-lous record
company willing to prey on the imagination and susceptibility of a generation
caught up in sixties nostalgia and desperate for an anti-hero. If so, it's working.

"Oh, for crying out loud," Juliet wailed. "Why
can't they just write about the music?"

Vince ignored her complaint and spoke to Luke.
"I was talking to the office in New York this
morning. There are T-shirts that say "Dennison
Lives" all over town. The mail's pouring in. Cults
are forming! There are wackos out there who
actually believe you're Luke Dennison!"

"You sound like you're happy about this," Juliet
accused.

"Hey, wackos buy records. We can use this to
our advantage. What do you think, Luke? Luke?"

"Yeah?"

"Have you been listening to me?" He moved
closer to Luke. "You look lousy."

"I'm tired."

Vince's expression switched from glee to
concern. "You're going onstage in an hour." He
studied Luke for another moment, then said,
"Come on down to my room. I'll give you
something."

"What?" Juliet asked.

But Vince and Luke were already walking out
the door.

168

* * *

Juliet stood in the wings and watched Luke do the last encore. All signs of exhaustion were gone. Luke was racing all over the stage, leaping, flailing his arms, with the look of a wild man out of control. Several times, he crashed into the others on the stage. They didn't look too pleased about his zeal.

He was high, that was clear to Juliet. And it wasn't Ecstasy this time. "What did you give him?" she asked Vince.

"Don't worry about it," Vince said.

"I have to worry about it," she snapped. "This is my job, remember? You wanted me to take care of him. Not to mention the fact that I love him, and you're sending him down the drain."

"He's not going down the drain," Vince replied. "He's heading right for the moon."

The song ended, with the final drumroll muffled by a blast of applause and cheers. The stage went dark, and the guys began stumbling off.

"What the hell were you doing out there?" Kyle yelled at Luke.

"Having fun. Making music. You should try it sometime."

"What's that supposed to mean?" Kyle demanded to know.

"You were a maniac out there," Josh complained.

Luke wasn't at all offended. "Yeah, well, maybe that what the world needs. More maniacs."

"You're talking like an idiot," Michael muttered.

He started to move past Luke, but he tripped and bumped into him. Luke shoved him.

Juliet watched nervously as Michael's face went red, and he came toward Luke. Behind her, the audience was still screaming. Steve jumped in between the guys. "They're not moving out there. Go do another encore."

"We've done everything we know," Gary told him.

"No, we haven't," Luke said suddenly. He grabbed Gary and muttered something. Gary stared at him, incredulous.

"But you said—"

"Get out there!" Steve yelled, pushing the guys in the direction of the stage.

Gary pulled the other musicians together and told them something. They went back out onstage. The lights came up, and the roar was shattering. Josh began a melody on the keyboards. The audience went nuts. It was a famous opening chord, one that anyone who had the slightest knowledge of rock music would recognize. It had been the number-one hit of 1968—and it had made Luke Dennison a star.

Desperately, Juliet prayed that her ears were deceiving her. But then Luke began to sing, and her heart sank.

Beside her, Vince rubbed his hands together. "Brilliant, brilliant. He's a genius."

"It's a gimmick," Juliet whispered. "He said he wouldn't do gimmicks." She made her way back to the dressing room and sat down. It's the drugs, she told herself. That's what's making him do this. That's not him out there, that's not my Luke.

Whoever he was, when he showed up back in the dressing room, his eyes were still unnaturally bright. "Come on, babe. We're going out."

Babe. He'd never called her that before. And she couldn't confront him about singing that song. He was obviously still speeding.

She rose unsteadily. "Luke, I don't want to go to any party."

"We're not going to a party. The guys are getting on my nerves. We're going dancing, just you and me."

She approached him tentatively. "Luke, I don't want to go dancing."

"Then I'll go by myself," he said.

She couldn't let him do that, not in his condition. "At least, change your clothes," she said. His T-shirt was streaked with dirt and sweat, and someone had torn the pocket off his jeans.

But he wouldn't. He practically dragged her from the room.

There was a limo waiting outside. "Take us to the hottest club in town," Luke ordered the driver. Juliet sat back and tried to stay calm. At least they had a car and a driver. Nothing too terrible could happen.

Luke fidgeted all the way. Upset and anxious, Juliet couldn't hold back. "Vince gave you speed, didn't he?"

"Don't start nagging me," Luke barked. "I needed something tonight. I couldn't go on without it."

171

"Why did you sing that song?"

"What is this, a cross-examination?" He stared at her, long and hard and steady, and then he answered her question. "Because it was in me to sing it, that's why. Now, shut up and leave me alone!"

She shrank back. Never, *never* had he spoken to her like that. Those other times, when she'd expressed her concern about the Ecstasy, the tequila, the chain-smoking, he hadn't raged at her. When he'd cried, that had been frightening, too, but she could put her arms around him. She was afraid to touch him right now. It wasn't her lover there, sitting next to her. It was a stranger.

The limousine pulled up in front of a long, low building with a wide walkway leading to it. There was a crowd of well-dressed people milling about, men in suits, women in cocktail dresses.

"Luke, this doesn't look like a place for us," Juliet said, but he was already out of the car. Moving through the crowd, she was grateful for the darkness. No one recognized him.

There was a thick gold rope blocking the entrance, and a burly man stood behind it. Luke put a hand on the rope to lift it, but the man shook his head. "Sorry, we've got a dress code. Coat and tie required."

"Let's go," Juliet said, but Luke wouldn't even look at her. He faced the man belligerently.

"Don't you know who I am?"

"I don't care if you're the Prince of Wales, buddy, you can't come in without a coat and tie."

172

"Don't call me buddy. I'm not your buddy."

Another even larger man approached. "You got problems here, Howie?"

"I don't know." The man turned back to Luke. "Have we got a problem or are you going to leave?"

"You're going to have a problem if you don't get out of my way," Luke threatened.

Juliet placed a trembling arm on his. He shook it off.

The larger man spoke ominously. "Sir, you'll have to leave." Luke didn't budge. Another couple came to the rope. The first man began to lift it. Luke grabbed it away from him.

"Look at me!" he yelled. "Who do you see?"

"I see someone who's not getting into this club," the man replied. He reached for the rope. Luke pushed him back.

"Okay, pal, let's go," the other man stated. He reached out to take Luke's arm.

What happened next was something out of a movie. Luke's hand formed a fist. It shot out and landed squarely against the man's jaw. The other man started blowing on a whistle. Out of nowhere, two police officers appeared. Then Luke was on the ground, pinned down.

Dimly, Juliet heard shrieking. She wasn't sure if the sound was coming from the whistle, from Luke, or from someone in the crowd. Or from herself.

CHAPTER · 14

Juliet had never been in a police station before. She sat stiffly in a hard chair, watching the swinging doors through which the police had taken Luke. They'd told her to wait here.

When she wasn't looking at the swinging doors, she was watching the entrance. She'd called Vince immediately after their arrival, and he'd said he was on his way. The clock on the wall told her that that had been a half hour ago.

Surreptitiously, she surveyed the others in the waiting room. It was not a happy-looking group. Two teenage girls were weeping, streams of mascara making black rivers down their faces. A man chain-smoked nervously. An older woman twisted a scarf in her hands while the man next to her patted her back. The air was thick with fear, tension, sadness. Juliet shared all their emotions.

The young man now entering the station certainly didn't look upset. If anything, he was positively jaunty as he strolled over to the reception desk and spoke to the sergeant there.

Juliet couldn't hear him, but he appeared to be asking for something. The sergeant shook his head. The man kept on talking in a low voice, but the sergeant continued to make negative signs.

Obviously frustrated, the man left the desk and gazed around the room. He spoke to the teenage girls, but whatever they told him didn't satisfy him. Then he came over to Juliet.

"Excuse me, did you see a guy brought in here, in his twenties, longish dark hair . . . "

Without thinking, Juliet said, "Luke?"

The man's face lit up. He sat down next to Juliet and whipped out a notebook. "Tell me what you saw. Did he look drunk? Was he in handcuffs?"

Juliet froze. "Who are you?"

"Joe Fleming, *Starlight Magazine*. What time did they bring Luke in? Did you hear what they were charging him with?"

Juliet was dangerously close to tears. "I don't know anything. Please, go away, leave me alone."

But her reaction only provoked the reporter's interest. "You the girlfriend? What's your name?"

She never thought she'd be so happy to see Steve and Vince. Vince went directly to the desk. Steve spotted Juliet, and came over to her.

"Where is he?"

Juliet nodded toward the swinging doors. The sergeant was directing Vince through them. The man next to her jumped up. "Who are you?"

"Steve Lindsay. I'm the manager of Incarnation."

"Steve!" Juliet cried in despair. "He's a reporter!"

That didn't seem to bother Steve. "You better

175

talk to Vince Shepard," he said. Vince returned and joined them. "It's okay, I can handle this. Steve, take her back to the hotel."

"I'm not going anywhere," Juliet declared hotly.

Vince took her aside. "Look, Juliet, I've got a lot of wheeling and dealing to do here, and you can't help. The best thing you can do is be there for him when I get him back to the hotel. Don't worry, I'll take care of everything." He sounded remarkably calm, even cheerful, given the situation.

Behind him, she could see Steve talking to the reporter. "Vince, that guy is from a magazine."

"Yeah, I figured. This is great press for us, it helps the whole image. You can't buy publicity like this. You go on now, okay?"

Shocked, Juliet didn't put up any more resistance. She allowed Steve to lead her out of the station and into a waiting taxi.

They rode in silence for a moment. "Don't you want to know what happened?" Juliet asked.

"I've got the gist of it. Some doorman wouldn't let Luke into a club, and Luke took a swing at him, right?"

"Yes, that's right. And do you know why Luke took a swing at him?"

"Because he was pissed off."

"Because he was high! Because Vince gave him speed before the concert!"

Steve sighed wearily. "Juliet, you saw the condition Luke was in this morning. He needed a little . . . stimulation if he was going to get on that stage."

176

His lack of concern infuriated her. "Haven't you noticed what it's doing to him? Don't you care?"

"I care about the band. Incarnation is going to be the biggest thing to hit the music scene in years. They're going places." He paused, and actually looked directly at Juliet. "You know the expression, Juliet. Sex, drugs, rock 'n' roll. That's the way it is. You're just going to have to deal with it."

There's more to it than that, she wanted to scream. Luke is changing, something's happening to him, and none of you seem to care!

But she said nothing. She was so tired, so depressed, she felt anything she said wouldn't make any sense. She needed to think, to figure out what was going on. She was the one who was supposed to be taking care of Luke. He was her responsibility.

Back in the hotel room, she took off her clothes and got into bed. But even before her head hit the pillow, she knew there was no way she'd sleep. She picked up the remote control and tried to find something on television, but nothing held her attention. She got up, went to the closet, and opened her suitcase.

The book was still there. She'd meant to leave it in one of the hotel rooms, but it had always slipped her mind. She picked it up and took it back to bed.

She turned to the center first, where the photos were. There he was, Luke Dennison, in a swaggering pose, with a cigarette dangling from his mouth. There were shots of him in performance with his band. In one of them, he was leaping, suspended

in air. There was a candid shot of Dennison
with his girlfriend, Gloria. He looked so much like
Luke there, Juliet thought. But Gloria—she held
the book closer and examined the girlfriend. No,
Gloria held no resemblance to *her*. But then, why
should she?

There were other photos, taken toward the end
of his brief life. His life style had taken its toll. His
eyes were glazed, unfocused, and his body was
bloated.

She turned back to the beginning and began to
read. The first few chapters were devoted to
Dennison's childhood and his background. She
skimmed through this part, skipping pages until
she came to the release of his album.

Much of what she read was common
knowledge—Dennison's use of drugs to fuel his
performance, his heavy drinking and incessant
partying. What she found more interesting were the
descriptions of his personality.

> Friends who knew him before his rise
> to fame described him as intense,
> thoughtful, and perceptive. As his sister
> said, "Luke had a way of looking at you,
> as if he could see right through to your
> innermost thoughts. And when he told
> you what those thoughts were, he was
> always right."

There were other comments from longtime
friends, affirming that Luke Dennison had been a

kind and gentle person. But as his fame grew, his personality seemed to change.

> During the band's tour, his behavior became erratic. At any hint of criticism or concern, he might weep, or, worse, go into a sudden and inexplicable rage. Childlike tantrums became routine. Yet despite his inconsistent and increasingly outlandish conduct, he retained his charisma. He attracted a wide variety of admirers, from serious music fans to one bizarre group who proclaimed him a god.

Grimacing, Juliet turned to another chapter, this one dealing with Dennison's problems with his band. She learned that their once-congenial relationship had rapidly deteriorated while the band was on the road.

> It's possible that the disproportionate attention Luke received from fans and the press sparked jealousy among the other band members. It is more likely that it was his reaction to the attention that created the dissension.
>
> As Dennison's antics on stage became more manic and reckless, the band members felt that their own performances suffered. Dennison began making irrational demands on them, ordering them to change musical arrangements at a

moment's notice or perform some number that wasn't a part of their repertoire. The first big confrontation came when he insisted that the keyboard player be fired for having the wrong "aura."

Juliet skipped around the book, picking sections at random and reading them. She wasn't sure what she was looking for—until she found it.

Dennison's first run-in with the law was only a hint of what was to come. While on tour in Minneapolis, he and Gloria tried to go to a then-fashionable disco. Dennison wasn't recognized by the doorman, and they were refused entrance due to his attire. High on amphetamines, Dennison flew into one of his rages and punched the doorman. He was promptly arrested.

She slammed the book shut and sat there, very still. We're not in Minneapolis, she told herself. But that knowledge did nothing to ease her mind.

The room felt like it was closing in on her. She jumped out of bed, put her clothes back on, and went downstairs.

The lobby of the hotel was quiet at one in the morning, but the cocktail lounge off to one side was open. When she went in, she saw Gary, sitting alone at the bar.

"Hi," she said, taking the seat next to him.

His responding smile seemed to take major effort on his part. "Is Luke back?"

"No. Do you think they'll keep him in jail?"

Gary shook his head. "Palladium will bail him out. Vince will probably be able to get them to drop the charges." Still, his expression was glum as he toyed with his drink.

"Vince didn't even seem upset when he came to the station," Juliet remarked.

Gary wasn't surprised. "He thinks it's good for Luke's image." He snorted. "Vince says the fans want dangerous rock stars."

Juliet took a deep breath. "You know, Luke Dennison did something like that once. Slugged a doorman at a nightclub."

Gary looked at her with mild interest. "Oh, yeah?" He smiled ruefully. "I'll bet that's why Vince is pleased. He's pushing this Dennison thing. And Luke's buying into it."

The bartender spoke. "What can I get for you?"

"Just water, please," Juliet said. She waited for it to arrive, and then took a big gulp, hoping it would reduce the lump in her throat. It had no effect at all. "Gary . . . do you think Luke hit that doorman because he knew Luke Dennison had done that once? I mean, is he acting like this on purpose?"

"I don't know," Gary replied. "He claims he doesn't know anything at all about Luke Dennison. But the way he's been acting lately . . . the other day I asked him not to run around so much onstage, because he practically knocked me over

181

at the concert in Charlottesville. He threw a tantrum, Juliet, just like a little kid."

"Dennison used to do that," Juliet said softly. "But that doesn't make sense, Gary. You know how he always hated it when people compared him to Luke Dennison. Why would he suddenly start acting like Luke Dennison on purpose?"

Gary took a long drink, then set the empty glass down. "Maybe he thinks he *is* Luke Dennison."

"Don't make jokes like that," Juliet burst out.

"I'm not making jokes." Gary pushed a lock of hair out of his tired eyes. "I don't know what's going on, Juliet. All I'm sure of is that he's making a lot of trouble for the rest of us. Especially Josh."

Juliet bit her lip. "What kind of trouble is he making for Josh?" With dread, she waited for what she knew he'd say.

"He wants Josh out of the band." He shook his head wearily. "Luke says Josh is sending out the wrong vibrations, whatever the hell that means."

"It's the drugs," Juliet whispered. "The drugs are making him act like that."

Gary gazed at her sadly. "He wants to act like that. The drugs just help."

Juliet hugged herself, trying to stop the shivers that seemed to be taking over her body. "What are we going to do?"

They talked for a long time, but they got nowhere. Nothing Gary said settled the disarray in her mind. But how could he help, when nothing that was happening made any sense?

Kyle came into the bar. "Luke's back, Juliet."

She ran to the elevator and went up to their floor. The door to the hotel suite was ajar, and Juliet went in. "Luke?"

The room was pitch-black, except for an eerie glow on the floor. As her eyes adjusted, she made out the shape of a bowl, and she could see wisps of smoke curling from it. There was the pungent odor of incense.

The glow flickered on the three figures sitting around the bowl. "Who are you? What are you doing here?"

"We were waiting. He let us in." The drowsy voice wasn't identifiable. Juliet moved closer. One of the figures, a woman, was swaying and chanting tunelessly.

"Luke let you in?" She thought one of them inclined a head. "Where is he?"

The bedroom door opened slowly. Luke stood there, leaning heavily against the doorjamb. Juliet went to him.

"Are you all right?"

He made a sign of assent.

"Who are those people?"

"They were waiting for me in the lobby." A crooked smile crossed his face. "My fan club."

"Tell them to leave."

"They don't want to leave."

Juliet moved swiftly and addressed the group. "Go away. Get out of here."

"We want to pray," a man murmured.

"Then go find a religion," Juliet snapped.

"We found one," he said. The woman spoke up.

"He's come back, you see. He's been resurrected."

Juliet fought back a wave of nausea. "Luke?"

With a glassy expression, Luke approached. He sat down on the floor, with his legs crossed and his arms outstretched. The man and the two women began crooning loudly.

"Stop it!" Juliet shrieked. "Stop it right now!"

But she might as well have been mute, invisible. Terror made her momentarily paralyzed. "Luke, let's get out of here."

"No," he said softly. "I have to stay."

"Then make them leave!" she cried.

"No," he said again.

She ran to the light switch and hit it, thinking the sudden brightness might shock him to his senses. But nothing changed. And now that she could see his face clearly, she was truly frightened. There was something in his expression she'd never seen before—an uncanny light in his eyes, a strange, transfixed smile on his face.

And when he spoke again, he didn't sound drugged. If anything, his tone was frighteningly calm and clear. "You see, they believe in me, Juliet. They know who I am. Do you?"

"No," she whispered.

He looked away. "Then maybe *you'd* better leave."

She fled into the bedroom, and she moved fast, so she wouldn't have to think. It didn't take long to pack her suitcase.

She carried it back out into the main room. "I'm leaving, Luke."

They were chanting loudly now, an off-key rendition of an old Luke Dennison song. At first, Juliet didn't think Luke had heard her.

He lifted his head slightly. He had to be aware of her standing there, suitcase in hand. But he said nothing at all.

And he did nothing to stop her as she walked out the door.

CHAPTER · 15

At least there was no line at the airport ticket counter. Unfortunately, there were no flights either.

"It's three A.M.," the ticket agent pointed out, unnecessarily. "Our next flight to Chicago is at seven, and it's completely booked." She checked her computer. "The earliest flight I can put you on is at 9:15."

"All right, I'll take that one," Juliet said.

"Will that be one-way or round-trip?"

"One-way."

"Do you have a seating preference?"

"No."

Silently, she congratulated herself for having had the foresight to obtain her own credit card before leaving on the tour. Palladium Records had assured her they would cover all expenses. But maybe, in the back of her mind, she'd known there would come a time when she'd have to take care of herself.

Ticket in hand, she went to the hotel reservation desk to secure a room for what was left of the night. A shuttle bus deposited her in front of the airport hotel. Within minutes, she was ensconced in an immaculately neat, clinically clean room. Plainly furnished in bland noncolors, it had a cold, sterile atmosphere. Which seemed highly appropriate to the way she was feeling—numb. Anesthetized. Like she'd left all emotion back at that suite downtown.

She knew she should go directly to sleep. She was exhausted, and she had to be up in a few hours for her flight. But the notion of being able to fall peacefully asleep struck her as ludicrous. She resigned herself to being up all night. Remote control in hand, she explored the television options.

Thank goodness for cable. Even at three in the morning, there was plenty to choose from. Movies. Reruns of old series. Comedians.

She settled on a local 24-hour news program that was reporting somberly on poverty in Atlanta. She needed to hear about people who had far greater problems than she had.

When that sequence was over, the anchorwoman turned to local news. "Earlier this evening, a confrontation occurred at Scruples, Atlanta's newest night spot. According to witnesses, the rock star known as Luke attempted to enter Scruples despite the fact that he did not meet the dress code of the club. Denied admittance, Luke attacked the doorman, and was promptly arrested by police. Our reporter caught up with the enigmatic rock star on his way out of the police station."

There was Luke, blinking rapidly as the cameras

flashed in his eyes. "What happened, Luke?" an unseen voice called out.

He only grinned foolishly. Vince broke in to answer for him. "Luke simply lost his temper, and he regrets any distress he's caused. Fortunately, the doorman has decided not to press charges."

"Was this just a stunt, Luke?" someone yelled out. "Is it true that you're trying to imitate the life of Luke Dennison?"

Juliet gripped the edge of the bed, waiting to watch Luke fly into a rage.

He didn't. He spoke slowly and calmly. "We can only do what fate requires of us."

"What does that mean, Luke? Do you think you *are* Luke Dennison?"

"I am who I am," he said. "I do what I have to do." At that point Vince hustled him away.

The anchorwoman reappeared on the screen, but Luke's image remained before Juliet's eyes. The numbness was beginning to wear off. Now, she was aware of pain, an ache that seemed to permeate every pore of her body.

"Luke," she moaned aloud. Fiercely, she fought back the desire to rush to him, right that minute, to cradle him in her arms, to touch his face, to press her body against his. She rose and began pacing the floor. What could she do to reinforce her decision? How could she sustain her resolve, not give in to her need for him? She needed some confirmation to convince herself that she'd done the right thing in leaving.

She opened her suitcase. She'd packed in such a

rush that nothing was folded or organized. She dug around along the edge until she felt the book, and pulled it out. Then she sat down on the bed, and began to read—about Gloria.

According to the biographer, little was known about Gloria before she and Luke met on a beach in California. From that moment on, they were inseparable. She was described as a pretty and lively young woman with a generous nature and a strong-willed spirit.

"She was totally and utterly devoted to Dennison," the book declared.

> For Luke, Gloria was an anchor, and she was the only person who didn't forsake him in the last months of his life. Friends have said that Gloria was the stronger of the two, that she was the only one capable of keeping Dennison even remotely linked to reality. In the end, however, Luke dragged her down with him. She surrendered to Luke's need for escape through acid and heroin. As she told one friend, drugs became the only means through which she could retain any sense of unity with him. When Luke's lifeless body was discovered in a Rome hotel room, Gloria was stretched over him, comatose. She was revived, but within two days of Luke's death, she, too, succumbed. Like Luke's, her death was officially described as an accidental

overdose, though most of their acquaintances felt certain that the over-dose was a conscious decision on Gloria's part and demonstrated her unwillingness to live without him.

Juliet closed the book. She didn't need to read anymore. She recalled the expression used to describe Gloria—strong-willed. But her life seemed to be a contradiction of that. How could she be strong-willed and still stay with this man? And not just stay with him, but willingly follow him into that abyss of drugs and degradation and, ultimately, death? It didn't make sense. And yet, in a disquieting, unnerving way, Juliet understood.

She had an overwhelming urge to talk to somebody. Not just anybody—someone who knew her, who understood her. For one insane moment, Keith's face popped into her head. What a bizarre notion, she thought, shaking herself violently to remove the image.

Dani—that's who she needed to talk to.

She fumbled through her handbag and pulled out the postcard of the Eiffel Tower. She looked at her watch. It would be almost ten in the morning in France. She went to the phone and began punching in the numbers.

It took awhile for the connection to be established. While she waited, she reread the card. Dani sounded happy and excited. She was living in some sort of student housing, and she'd already made friends.

190

The phone began to ring, and a French-speaking voice responded. Quickly, Juliet tried to recall her high-school French. "Uh, bonjour, s'il vous plait, je voudrais parler avec Dani Feldman."

Her request was met with a babble of French so rapid that Juliet didn't have the slightest idea what the person was saying. But since the connection wasn't broken, she could only assume and hope that Dani was being fetched.

When she finally heard that familiar voice, she wanted to weep with joy. "Dani, it's me."

"Juliet! It's so great to hear from you! How's the tour going? I can't believe how big Incarnation is getting. Their songs are on the radio here!"

"Really? In France? That's great."

Dani's tone changed abruptly. "What's wrong?"

Amazing. Thousands of miles away, over a telephone line, Dani could still interpret Juliet's state of mind from just a few words.

"It's . . . it's Luke. I don't know where to begin."

"Begin at the beginning," Dani replied.

So she did. She told Dani the whole story, everything that had happened since she'd left Chicago. She described his mood swings, his behavior, his performances. She told her about the drugs, the weird fans, the incident at the nightclub.

When she was through pouring it all out, she was drained. Dani was silent for so long, she thought they'd been disconnected. "Dani?" she asked anxiously. "Are you there?"

"I'm here. Where are you now?"

"In a hotel at the airport. I've got a 9:15 flight."

"So you're deserting him."

Juliet gasped. "Dani, how can you put it that way? Haven't you been listening to me?"

"I've been listening. Luke's in trouble, and you're running away. How can you leave him when he obviously needs you so desperately?"

"I can't help him, Dani."

"You don't know that. You're all he has, Juliet."

"But don't you understand?" Juliet cried out. "He's acting like Luke Dennison, like he wants to relive Dennison's life! And you know what happened to him!"

"But he's *not* Luke Dennison." There was a pause, and then Dani asked, "Is he?"

"Don't be silly," Juliet said automatically, but she wished her response carried more conviction.

"And don't you be so narrow-minded," Dani said. "There are people, intelligent people, who believe in reincarnation. There are entire religions that are based on it."

Luke, as a reincarnation of a dead rock star. Living the same life again. With the same fate. She couldn't deny that the idea had crossed her mind, but the notion was so farfetched. It was easier to blame everything on the drugs, or the amnesia, or emotional instability . . . or even to believe that he was acting this way intentionally, to gain publicity.

"Dani, I don't know what he is or who he is, and I don't know if he knows anymore than I do. It doesn't matter, anyway. Dani, I'm frightened. I'm frightened for him and for myself, too. You know what happened to Gloria, Dennison's girlfriend, don't you?"

192

"But you're not Gloria. That's something we can be sure of. Jules . . . do you still love him? Jules? Are you there?"

"Yes," she replied dully. "Yes, I still love him. Oh, Dani, I love him so much, it's tearing me up inside." And then she was sobbing. "The thought of a life without him, it's . . . it's unthinkable. I know that deep inside he's still Luke, he's *my* Luke, but I can feel him disappearing, vanishing into some fantasyland . . ."

"Then pull him back! You can do it, Jules, you've got so much strength, enough for the both of you. You *can* save him. And if you truly love him, you will."

She wanted to believe Dani. Desperately, in her heart and soul and mind, she absorbed her words and held on to them tightly. All she really needed was the tiniest glimmer of hope, a hint that there was a chance.

So as Dani continued speaking of steadfast loyalty and devotion, she banished from her mind that last scene in the hotel suite and every other frightening moment. She drummed up images of the good times, the loving times, and she concentrated on remembering them. And by the time they finished their conversation, she was ready.

"You'll let me know what happens?" Dani asked.

"Yes, yes, of course." Now that she'd made a decision, she was anxious to follow through. But her natural courtesy forced her to ask, "How do you like being in France?"

"It's great, I'll write you all about it. Now you go do what you have to do."

What I have to do, she echoed silently as she hung up the phone. It was the same expression Luke had used on the TV news. It was like a sign.

She closed her suitcase and went to the door. Looking back, her eyes lit on the book, still lying on the bed. She started back for it and then stopped. Perhaps it would be better to leave it behind.

She checked out and called a taxi. The streets were deserted, and she was back at the downtown hotel quickly. She moved with determination through the empty lobby and onto the elevator. She had no idea what she'd find in the suite. Would the Church of Luke still be in session?

She had left her key behind, so she rapped on the door. It was probably a useless gesture. Luke was most likely passed out in there. She'd have to go back down to the lobby and get another key.

But that turned out not to be necessary. Luke opened the door.

He stood there, gazing at her as if she were some sort of alien being. But at least he appeared to be sober.

"You're back," he said softly.

"Yes."

He stepped aside and let her enter. She dropped her suitcase. "Luke," she began, but he put a finger to her lips.

"No, don't say anything. Just . . . just hold me."

She buried herself in his chest. He stroked her

hair. "I thought I'd never see you again," he said. "I wanted to die."

"Don't say that," she murmured.

"What happened tonight—"

"Let's not talk about it," she said.

"I couldn't help myself, you know. Hitting that doorman. It was inside me to do that. Everything I do . . . it's meant to be. I don't have any choice." His voice was trembling.

"You have a choice," Juliet cried fiercely.

"Help me, Juliet." His voice cracked. "Help me!"

He clung to her as if for dear life. Then they were on the floor, exchanging frantic, savage kisses. He stroked her furiously, and she responded with an impassioned fervor. The fire within her had never before blazed so violently. She was out of control, with no urge to resist her impulses. She held nothing back, for everything she had, everything she was, it was all his, too. And for this precious moment, this dear, beautiful instant, he belonged to her.

* * *

They were greeted the next day with the delivery of champagne and flowers and the news that Incarnation's album had officially gone platinum. It was number one on the charts, and all evidence indicated that it would be staying there for some time. A huge budget had been established for the next video. *Rolling Stone* would be doing a cover story. Plans for a European tour were in the works.

195

Steve, Vince, and the band members gathered in their suite. Food was ordered from room service, champagne bottles were popped, and it was a party.

Luke was laughing and joking, and not drinking too much, Juliet noted. She watched him in happy amazement as he caroused with the others like any bunch of buddies who had just hit the big time. All those terrifying possibilities—reincarnation, destiny, whatever—they seemed ridiculous now, like notions produced by an overactive and hysterical imagination, like concepts for a horror movie.

Vince was beaming at them all, rubbing his hands together gleefully. "And did I happen to mention there's a battle going on between the *Tonight Show* and *Letterman* over who's getting you guys on?"

While the guys were cheering that news, the phone rang. Vince picked it up. "Yeah?" Then he laughed. "You're putting me on, right? No kidding, really? Well, there's nothing I can do about it. Call the cops if it's bothering you." He hung up.

"What was that all about?" Gary asked.

"That was the hotel manager. He says there's a big crowd outside blocking the entrance to the hotel. He thinks it's got something to do with us."

"Yeah?" Gary went to the window. "You can't see the front of the hotel from here."

"You can from my room," Josh told them. "And I've got a balcony."

Champagne bottles in hand, they all trooped

down the hall. Josh made it to the window first. "Wow! Get a load of this!"

They all ran over to look. Juliet couldn't even estimate the size of the crowd gathered outside. Josh opened the balcony door, and now they could hear the cry of the mob.

"We want Luke! We want Luke!"

Gary rolled his eyes. "I guess every band has to have its resident heartthrob."

"Get out there, Luke," Steve urged. "Give them a thrill."

A sudden apprehension filled Juliet. "Luke, don't."

But he was already stepping out on the balcony. Shrill screams rose up to greet him. And a banner was unfurled.

As high up as they were, the words had been painted so huge that they could read them easily. "Luke Lives Again."

Juliet steeled herself to look at Luke. He was staring down at the banner, and his expression was neither angry nor upset. All Juliet could see on his face was a sweet, sad smile of resignation.

CHAPTER · 16

She could hear them fighting from way down the hall, through a closed door. Juliet couldn't make out the actual words, but she recognized the sounds of argument.

She was in the ladies' room of Palladium Records's Los Angeles offices. Incarnation was meeting with some company people to discuss plans for the next video.

She was startled by her own reflection in the mirror over the sink. The past three weeks had taken their toll. Her eyes were sunken, ringed with dark circles. She was pale, and her face seemed thin. She tried to repair some of the damage with makeup.

Three weeks. Was that really how long it had been since Atlanta? It seemed like an eon . . . or five minutes.

There had been some good times. One stood out in her mind. The band had performed in Austin, Texas. After the concert she and Luke had gone out to explore Austin's lively music scene, visiting clubs where fresh new talent was on display. At each place Luke was recognized and welcomed by young, friendly Texans. At one particular joint, the performing band begged him to jam with them, and he did. He sang "Tattoo," at a slower tempo, directly into Juliet's eyes, and the love he communicated was undeniable.

That night, they'd been so close, so connected. It was a memory she held on to tightly. She *had* to, in the hope that it would block out the other times he didn't want to remember at all. Like the night on stage when he started smashing equipment. Or the time he stopped singing in the middle of a number and began ranting and raving about the end of the world. And each time, the audience cheered and screamed and urged him on. These were Luke Dennison stunts, and they loved it.

Then there were the offstage moments of madness. Like the time he started a fire at a postperformance party. Or the night he sat on the ledge of a hotel window and declared his intention to jump.

Each and every time, the others—the guys in the band, Vince, Steve—had been helpless in trying to calm him down. Only Juliet had been able to get through to him. But she was beginning to wonder how much longer her powers of persuasion would hold up. She was so tired. At that very moment, she wanted nothing more than to lie down on the cold, hard tile of the restroom and let the darkness of sleep take her away from the darkness of reality.

But she had responsibilities out there. Dropping

her makeup pouch into her handbag, she left the restroom. Steve was in the hallway, pacing. When he saw Juliet, he waved her over with an air of immense relief.

"There you are! We need you. You have to talk to him. You're the only one he listens to."

A wave of fatigue passed through her. How many times in the past few weeks had she heard this? "What's the problem?"

"He won't go along with the video plans. He's got some insane idea . . ." He clutched his head. "Everything's going so well, and he wants to screw it all up. He's going off the deep end."

"Isn't this what you wanted, Steve?" she asked softly. "A wild and crazy rock star? A new Luke Dennison?"

Steve grimaced. "I'm beginning to think he believes his own publicity. But it's just an image, Juliet. He's acting like he *is* Luke Dennison."

Juliet didn't know whether to laugh or cry. Had it really taken Steve this long to figure it all out?

As she followed him down the hall, once again, she conjured up the memory of that night in Austin. There was another time, in New Orleans, when they'd strolled at dawn along the Mississippi River. And a good evening in Memphis . . .

But between those few times, when they were able to talk and share and express their love, were the other times. The times when he raged, the times when he brooded, the times he was too zonked out on something or other to do anything at all.

Even in the worst of times, she hadn't thought of leaving again. She'd made a commitment to him, for better or worse, and she was determined to hold on. But with each of those episodes, she could sense him moving farther and farther away from her. It was killing her.

It dawned on her that the angry voices had died down. She opened the door to the meeting room and went in.

The band members, Vince, and a couple of record company executives sat around a conference table. They were all quiet now, but she could see from their faces that nothing had been resolved. Gary's lips were pressed together in a tight, white line. Vince was rapping a pencil on the table.

It was unnerving for her to see how the boys lit up when she came in. Like Steve, they, too, had come to believe she had some special insight, some unique way of accessing the dark canyons of Luke's mind.

Even Vince seemed glad to see her. "Juliet, do you know about this?"

"About what?"

"Luke's idea for a music video."

"She doesn't," Luke said. "I only dreamed it this morning."

Out of the corner of her eye, she saw the two executives exchange sardonic smirks. She slipped into the empty chair next to Luke.

He shifted his chair to face her. He spoke to her, and her alone, as he proposed his vision of Incarnation's next video.

What he described was some sort of rapid sequence of images— explosions, eruptions, fires, scenes of devastation. The band itself would not appear at all. He implied that the scenes would produce some vivid, significant message.

It was probably brilliant, Juliet thought. It could well be a work of artistic genius. Maybe none of the others could comprehend it, and she wasn't surprised. Because all it sounded like to her was a bizarre, incoherent melange of unrelated, disjointed pictures.

When Luke finished, she was at a loss to come up with an appropriate response. One of the executives spoke up.

"Fabulous, Luke, absolutely fabulous. But it's not what the kids are going to want to watch. They want to see *you*."

"And the rest of you guys, of course," the other man added quickly.

Luke paid no attention to their remarks. "What do you think?" he asked Juliet.

She struggled to penetrate his mind, to comprehend the meaning, the motivation. "It's dramatic," she began carefully. "It's . . . it's . . . ." But she felt like her brain had ceased to function. "I'm not sure I understand it," she said.

Luke bowed his head. She had let him down, she could see that.

The tense silence in the room was broken when Steve burst in with a video cassette in hand. "I've got a preview of the Jerry Corbin show you taped yesterday," he announced.

"Let's take a look," Vince said, nodding toward a TV monitor and VCR set up in a corner of the room.

Everyone moved their seats so they could view the screen. Steve turned it on, inserted the cassette, and hit the play button. After a few seconds, the familiar face of the popular talk show host came on the screen. He made a few corny jokes and then introduced Incarnation.

The band performed the latest single from the album. When they finished, Corbin joined them. "Great job, fellows. Now, who's who?" He moved around and spoke briefly to each of the guys.

"And you must be the infamous Luke," he said with a jovial smile.

Luke appeared to be amused by that description. "Infamous," he said. "As in 'disreputable, scandalous, notorious—contemptible'?"

The host chuckled uneasily. "Well, I wouldn't say that."

"*I* would."

The camera moved in for a close-up. Luke's enigmatic smile didn't waver.

"Judging from your popularity, it certainly doesn't look like your fans are holding you in contempt," Corbin said.

"Oh, but they do," Luke said. "It's human nature to be fascinated by what you despise. Even when we hate ourselves, we look into mirrors. I am a mirror, and I show people what they don't want to see. But they keep looking."

"Didn't Luke Dennison once say something like that about himself?" Corbin asked.

203

"*I* said that." Luke turned, so that he was speaking directly into the camera. "I'm everything you fear, all those dark, ugly secrets you try to hide. I absorb your self-loathing. I show you the truth."

The screen went blank. Juliet looked around the room. Reactions ranged from disbelief to disgust. One of the executives drummed his fingers on the table. "I think we can give this Dennison thing a rest now."

"Of course, they're going to edit most of that out," Steve assured them.

"Of course," Luke murmured.

The other executive spoke. "I say we kill the whole Dennison angle."

"It's not an angle," Luke said.

"What the hell are you talking about?" Vince asked.

"Figure it out, man. You can't be that dense." He rose. "You can't stop me, you know. The people won't let you. It's in the stars. It's predestined."

"What's in the stars?" an executive asked in bewilderment.

"Think about it," Luke replied. He stalked out of the room.

Vince turned to Gary. "What's he on?"

"Nothing," Gary replied in a tired voice. "He's clean."

Juliet could vouch for that. She'd been with him all day. He was cold sober. That was small comfort. It made everything he said that much more disturbing.

She got up and went out. Luke was leaning against the wall, smoking a cigarette. "Come here," he said. She did, and he put his arm around her. "You don't get it, do you?" he asked sadly.

"I'm trying, Luke. Really, I'm trying. What's happening to us?"

He pulled her closer. "There's a gap between us, Juliet. It's getting wider."

He was right. And the knowledge of that was agony to her. She pressed her head against his chest, wishing that physical closeness could translate into some deeper connection.

"Is that what you want?" he asked. "A gap?"

"No!" she said fervently. "There shouldn't be any space between us. But I can't read your mind! I can't understand what you're thinking, where you're going." Her voice dropped to a whisper. "Maybe I'm not capable of understanding."

"You're the only one who could," he said.

"I *want* to understand."

"Do you, Juliet? Do you really?"

"Yes," she breathed. "Yes. Help me understand, Luke."

"I will," he said. "Tonight. After the concert. We'll be alone. We'll be together in a way we've never been before. And then you'll understand." He paused. "Do you believe in me?"

"Of course I believe you."

"No, I asked, do you believe *in* me? Do you believe who I am?"

She knew what he meant by that. But she didn't know how to respond.

"I love you," she said helplessly. That was all she could say in total honesty. She didn't know if it would be enough.

CHAPTER · 17

The backstage area of the modern entertainment complex had remarkably good insulation. Only faint echoes of what was going on in the performance arena could be heard.

Juliet sat in a lounge with people from Palladium and watched the band on closed-circuit television. She'd heard these songs so many times, she thought she'd become immune to their power. But listening to Luke tonight, even from a distance, she remembered that first time at Barney's, how his words had elevated her heartbeat, how her desire for him had blossomed.

Gazing at the screen, she could feel the old longing intensify.

She wasn't the only one to feel it. Women rushed the stage, only to be immediately hauled off by guards and roadies. That didn't discourage others from trying.

"Crazy kids," someone in the room remarked.

But another executive seemed to understand the crowd's reactions. "The guy's magic. They want to touch him, to feel it. They want to know if he's real."

Juliet turned to them. "Of course he's real! What do they think he is, some sort of fantasy?"

The others seemed startled by her outburst. But they were distracted when one of the group cried out, "Look!"

Juliet turned back to the screen. Luke had stopped singing in the middle of a song. He was clutching his head. Then, without warning, he suddenly leaped off the stage and dived into the audience.

She stood up and didn't bother to stifle her scream. Frozen in horror, she stared at the screen. Then, he reappeared, his form on the shoulders of fans who hoisted him back onto the stage.

She sat down, still breathing hard. She turned to see how the others in the room were reacting.

A couple of them looked alarmed, but one man spoke almost nonchalantly. "Luke Dennison used to do that at all his concerts," he commented.

As if in verification of that, the audience had begun to chant, "Dennison, Dennison, Dennison." Luke stood there, his arms outstretched, acknowledging them.

"So what's the deal with this guy?" another man asked. "Is he a reincarnation of Luke Dennison or just your basic raving lunatic?"

The first man chuckled. "Well, if he *is* Luke Dennison, we'd better get those guys back in the recording studio fast if we want another album. He may not be long for this world."

Juliet was appalled. "How can you talk about him like that?" she burst out.

A woman gazed at her kindly. "You're his girlfriend, right?"

Dumbly, Juliet nodded.

"Better watch out for him," the woman said. "I remember Luke Dennison. I don't know what's going on in your boyfriend's mind, but from what I've heard, he's on a mission to self-destruct."

Juliet nodded again. She could hear the words of Steve, Vince, and that old hippie back in New York. Take care of him. But how, when she didn't know what was going on in his mind either?

Toward the end of the concert, the audience went out of control. They broke through the barrier of guards. Incarnation was rushed off the stage just in time, before they could be trampled.

Juliet hurried out to meet Luke. Without a word, he took her hand and led her to an exit. A car awaited them. He gave some instructions to the driver, and got into the backseat with her.

"Where are we going?" she asked.

"It's a surprise," he said. He leaned back in the seat and closed his eyes.

They rode in silence for quite a while, leaving the downtown Los Angeles area and meandering through suburban neighborhoods. Luke didn't open his eyes again until the car stopped.

They got out and he took her hand and began walking. Juliet sniffed. There was the smell of salt in the air. A beach came into view.

"This is Venice Beach," Luke told her.

The name rang a distant bell in her memory. As they walked onto the beach, she took off her shoes and felt the sand between her toes.

Finally, Luke stopped walking. He sat down on the sand, and pulled Juliet down with him. He removed his shoes.

Was this it, she wondered. Did he think that making love on the beach would be the key to renewing their relationship?

But Luke made no gestures to suggest that intention. He lit a cigarette and gazed out at the water. "This is where it started, you know," he said. "This is where it all began."

Then she remembered why she knew the name of the beach. Luke Dennison and Gloria—this was where they met.

"Did you read my book, Luke? Is that how you knew about this place?"

"No." He looked at her. "You still don't understand, do you? You're afraid to believe the truth."

A powerful shiver raced through her. "Tell me, Luke. What's the truth?"

"I know who I am. And so do you. You just haven't accepted it."

"Luke Dennison is dead," she cried out.

"Maybe," Luke said. "Maybe not. His spirit lives in me, Juliet. Can you understand that?"

"I'm trying," she said brokenly. "I don't know if I can accept this."

"No," he said. "No, you can't, not like this." He brushed a lock of hair from her forehead. "Not with all those doubts. I can help you lose them. If you trust me. Do you trust me?"

"I love you. I have to trust you."

He reached into his pocket and took out a wad of tissue. Unwrapping it, he revealed two small pills. She gazed at them in a sort of horrified fascination.

"I'd never hurt you," he said. "I just want you to feel what I'm feeling, see what I'm seeing. I want to open your mind, so you can accept me."

She believed him. She knew he couldn't hurt her. And if this pill—acid, speed, whatever it was— could bring them closer, it was worth the risk. With a trembling hand, she took one of the pills. He took the other.

Wrapping her arms around her knees, she waited. After a few moments, she wondered if there had been anything in that pill at all. Nothing was happening to her.

But she was utterly, totally relaxed. And she wasn't frightened, not in the least. It's nice here, she thought, in the warm cloak of darkness, breathing the salty air, listening to the soft murmur of the waves. The waves . . . suddenly she had an enormous desire to feel the cold tingle of the water.

She rose, and walked a few yards to the edge of the water, just close enough so the water could lap at her feet. It was a lovely sensation. And the way the waves moved, forward, then receding, and the frothy foam . . . remarkable. Returning, she noted with interest that she didn't have to walk. She could float, just above the sand.

Luke was watching her, smiling. "You're so beautiful."

"So are you," she promptly replied. She sat down next to him, and ran her fingers through his hair. How silky it is, she thought. Had she ever noticed that before? His skin, she marveled at its softness. And those eyes . . . she uttered a soft gasp.

"Luke, I can see myself in your eyes!"

"Of course you can," he said. "That's the you in me, looking out."

"Of course," she echoed. It made perfect sense.

"What do you see, from inside me?" he asked.

"I see—me!" She started to giggle, but then she stopped. She saw something else. Danger. Fear. She placed a reassuring hand on his. "I'm going to help you, Luke. I'm going to set you free."

"You can't save me, Juliet. There's a plan for me. I have a destiny. You know that, you read the book."

She shook her head violently. "But my love is stronger than any destiny. I can fight it."

"Don't fight for me. Come with me."

"Where to?"

"Everywhere. Above and beyond."

"And how are we going to get there?" she asked.

"We're going to fly, you and me. And keep flying."

"Forever," she said.

"No, not forever," he corrected her. "But it will be extraordinary, while it lasts. Will you come with me?"

"I don't have a choice, do I? If it's our destiny—"

"*My* destiny. I want you to be a part of it. But you have a choice."

She knew better. It was all very clear now. "We're bound together, Luke. I have no choice."

His eyes lit up with pleasure. "You *do* understand!"

She could envision it all, with a crystal clarity. To fly with him, to reach dazzling heights of joy, fused together in a splendid harmony . . . "We'll touch the stars, Luke." She clutched his arm in excitement. "Luke, look. There are stars in the water! We can touch them now."

"Now?"

"Yes!" She got up. How light she was! The slightest gust of wind could blow her away. She reached down and grabbed Luke's hand. She wasn't going to leave him behind.

He rose, and they drifted to the water's edge. They began to walk into the sea. The water crept up her legs, lapping at her thighs. Soon it was at her waist. It felt odd, to be half wet. She wanted to be covered completely. Then they could float, into oblivion. Why wait? At least they'd go there together. Together. Not like Gloria, who had to go alone.

Then she stopped. "I hear something."

"Don't look back," Luke said.

But the voice was so strangely familiar. She turned.

"What are you seeing?"

How odd, she thought. "It's me."

213

"What is Juliet doing on the beach?" Luke asked. "Waving good-bye?"

"No. She's calling me back." In slow motion, she started toward the shore. "I have to find out what I want."

He didn't try to stop her. She gripped his hand, pulling him back with her. He was so heavy, her arm ached from the strain.

They stumbled out of the water. Her eyes searched the beach. "Where am I?" she wailed.

"In me," he said. "In me, remember?" He pulled her toward him, and they both fell back onto the sand. She knelt over him, and searched his eyes for her reflection.

"I can't see myself now!" But of course she couldn't. How could she be in him, when she was out on this beach somewhere?

Fear gripped her, it choked her like a noose. "I'm lost!" she cried out. "Where is Juliet? I have to find her!" She tried to scramble to her feet but Luke held her down.

"Stay with me," he pleaded. "Fly away with me."

"I don't know how to fly, Luke," she wept. "And neither do you."

"Then we'll crash. But we'll crash together."

Crazy jigsaw puzzle pieces appeared in her mind. They started to interlock, one piece at a time.

To be his Gloria . . . to keep him company until the end, an end that couldn't be very far away, if he was really carrying the life force of Luke Dennison in him. If that was his destiny.

214

And even if it wasn't, he believed in it so strongly, he'd make it happen. And where did she fit in? It was a piece of the jigsaw puzzle that was missing. Maybe because she wasn't supposed to be in the puzzle at all. It was Gloria in the picture. Not Juliet.

"Juliet," she said aloud. "If I stay with you, I'll lose Juliet. She'll be gone forever."

"You don't need her. You can live through me."

And die through you, she finished silently. The panic was gone. All that remained was an immense, overwhelming sadness.

"Luke, I can't save you, can I?"

"No."

"I think . . . I have to save myself."

A curtain came down over his eyes.

"Come with me," she asked, but she knew her request was in vain.

"I can't," he said, with a finality that couldn't be argued. "There are things I'm supposed to do."

"Maybe there are things *I'm* supposed to do, too."

She'd wanted to share his feelings, and now she did. His despair was as real to her as her own.

"You'd better go," he said. "You have to find Juliet. She's lost."

"No, not lost. She's waiting. She can wait a little longer."

"How much longer?"

She turned her anguished eyes to meet his. "Long enough to say good-bye."

He took her in his arms for what she knew

215

would be the last time. Their tears mingled together as they touched and kissed and shared body and soul. This was only going to make it harder to leave, she knew that. But she needed him, she had to have his love, for this one ultimate, precious moment.

To make a memory that would last a lifetime.

CHAPTER · 18

The famous Chicago wind was asserting itself that December afternoon. It couldn't penetrate Juliet's heavy parka, but she shoved her gloved hands into her pockets for additional protection.

Dani, on the other hand, was hopping up and down in an effort to keep warm. Her jacket was too thin.

"Do you want to wait in the car?" Juliet asked. "I won't stay much longer."

"No, that's okay," Dani said. "I should have worn a warmer coat. I forgot how cold it gets here in December."

"Isn't it cold in Paris now?"

"Oh, sure, but we don't have a wind like this. I guess you feel it more right here. There are no big buildings to block it."

She was right. The highest structures in the cemetery were some rather grand monuments that marked some family graves.

The grave that they were facing had no fancy monument. All it held was a plain, granite square.

217

On all the surrounding stones, there were names, two dates, and a reference to the late person's relationships—beloved son, beloved mother, that sort of thing. This stone displayed only one word, a name, and not even a full name. Only one date. And there was no clue as to who might have been left behind.

"Beloved," Juliet murmured under her breath.

Dani moved closer. "They should have put up a statue, a bust or something like that."

Juliet shrugged. "It would have been stolen by some fanatic groupie."

"Like Luke Dennison's, in Rome," Dani commented. "The bust is gone, and the stone's covered with graffiti."

Juliet suspected this one would be, too, in a very short time.

"I'm sorry I couldn't be here for the funeral," Dani apologized. "I couldn't leave Paris till the Christmas holidays started."

Juliet grimaced. "It was awful. A real media event. I think Palladium was using it to promote the new album."

"It was recorded in London, wasn't it?"

She nodded. "When Gary was here for the funeral, he asked if I wanted to hear the tapes."

"Did you?"

"No. I'm not ready for that, yet."

Dani spoke hesitantly. "How did he die, Juliet? You hear so many stories . . ."

"The official story is some sort of heart problem. Steve, the band's manager, called me from London."

218

She remembered picking up the phone, hearing Steve's voice, and knowing what he was about to tell her. She wondered if Steve had been shocked by the matter-of-fact way she accepted the news.

She smiled slightly. "Of course, a lot of people don't believe he's really dead. The tabloids have already started to report sightings."

"Luke Dennison all over again," Dani remarked. "Juliet, do you think—"

"He's dead," Juliet declared flatly. "It doesn't matter who he was."

Dani was hugging herself. "You *are* cold," Juliet said. "Go wait in the car. I'll be right there."

"Okay, if you're sure you don't mind."

But once she was gone, Juliet wasn't sure why she'd wanted a moment alone. It wasn't as if she felt she could have some special communication with him here. The stone, the grave, the casket that lay beneath the earth . . . they had nothing to do with Luke.

So she just stood there and stared at his name. She'd never seen him again after that night on Venice Beach. Oh, she'd caught glimpses of him once in a while on television, and occasionally a photo appeared in a popular magazine. Every now and then, she'd hear or read about some incident he was involved in. An onstage riot in San Francisco. A brawl in Seattle.

Had he found his Gloria, she wondered. Was he alone when he descended into his destiny?

Had he touched the stars? Or did he merely teeter on the edge of oblivion, until he lost his balance? And, at the end, did he think of her at all?

He'd lived out his destiny, just as he'd said he would. Maybe that was why she didn't cry when she got the news. She'd been expecting it for so long. It was almost a relief. She could let go now.

If *he* would. If he would only stop creeping into her head, invading her mind.

"Let me go, Luke," she whispered.

"Juliet."

She froze. For one insane moment, she thought the voice was coming from the grave. But it was coming from behind her. She turned. "Keith!"

He came toward her. "I hope I'm not disturbing you."

"No, not at all."

"I read about Luke. I'm sorry, Juliet."

"Thank you." She gazed at him. "It's been a long time, Keith."

"Nine months," he said. "Two weeks, three days . . ."

She smiled. "You look good."

"So do you."

There was an awkward silence. "How did you know I was here?"

"Just took a chance. I called you at your father's—"

"I don't live there anymore. I thought he and Eleanor needed some privacy, and I . . . I just felt like I couldn't go back to the same life."

"Where are you living now?"

"In a dorm. I'm at the university now."

"You still planning on going into anthropology?"

220

"I don't know. I haven't really decided what I want to do. I'm just sort of playing it by ear, I guess."

"That's a switch," Keith remarked. "You always seemed to have your life planned."

She turned back to face the grave. "I've changed."

"You must miss him," he said quietly.

"Yes," she said. "I miss him." It seemed to her to be such an inadequate expression.

"If you ever want to talk about it . . ."

"Someday, maybe. I should go now. Dani's waiting in the car."

"I'll walk you there, if it's okay."

"Of course. Just a minute."

But her eyes lingered on the grave. There are no ghosts, Juliet, she told herself. Get on with your life.

But Luke was a part of her life now. He was a part of who she was. Moments before, she'd asked him to let her go. But that was a futile request. *She* was the one holding on.

Was she a different person because of Luke, she wondered. Yes. And no. He had touched her, and he had released her spirit. He had set her free, to soar, to explore, to feel.

But she was still Juliet. She could care now, truly care, and yet not be consumed by her caring. She could give of herself, but not give herself away. Because of Luke, she had loved. Because of Juliet, she had survived.

And she would love again. Not like she'd loved

Luke, though. It was too dangerous. She'd gone as close to the sun as she dared. But she'd never regret knowing that love.

She could turn away now. Silently, she started up the path with Keith. His hand felt reassuring, comforting. It would be nice to spend some time with him. Maybe, who knew, something might even start up between them again. It wasn't an unappealing thought.

But he'd have to accept that there would always be a part of her forever looking back.

A.G. Cascone

IN A CROOKED LITTLE HOUSE

. . . lived a twisted little man

People are dying at Huntington Prep. A fall down the stairs, a drowning, a fatal bump on the head. It could happen anywhere. But Iggy-Boy knows these aren't accidents. Now he's set his sights on beautiful Casey, the nicest girl in school. She's in terrible danger, but she doesn't know it. She doesn't even know Iggy-Boy exists. But Iggy-Boy is someone she knows, someone nearby, someone who's watching her every move . . .

0-8167-3532-8 • $3.50